BURIED

TRUTHS

BURIED

TRUTHS

The Summersville Series
BOOK 3

MCCAID PAUL

Cover Illustration by © 2019 Damonza

Edited by Josh Vogt

Book formatting by SGR-P Formatting Services www.sgr-pub.com/services

ISBN-13: 978-0999614570

To my grandparents,

For your support and many life lessons.

I love you.

CONTENTS

The woman is known for her smile.

Not for her eyes. Not for her hair. That's something only a daughter knows.

She smiles from her little girl's dresser, in a field of dandelions, absorbing the beauty around her. It's the only image the girl has of her mother, one ingrained memory, living in her deepest, darkest thoughts.

It's best to know that she's smiling. To think she's the happiest woman in the world.

Because for Billie, it's easier to believe a lie.

PROLOGUE

5 Years Ago

THE NIGHT WAS full of lies.

Moonlight streamed in through the open window, revealing a pathway as Candice Hagen hurried down the small, spiral staircase.

"I'm fine," she called back, her voice drifting to the top where her husband stood.

John Hagen's eyes followed his wife. Her lie rang in his ears. He watched her closely, inspecting her every move.

She wasn't fine. Not tonight, at least. He spotted it in her walk, could see it etched on her face like a menacing scar. Her words dripped with it.

A seven-year-old Billie stood waiting for her mother

at the bottom of the staircase, face scrunched up in a frown. "I don't want you to go," she whined.

"It's okay, honey. Emily will watch out for you while I'm gone." She motioned toward the young woman standing in the doorway. "We'll be back before you know it."

John Hagen studied his daughter, her eyes glistening with fresh tears, a stuffed, furry monkey clutched to her chest. Billie looked so small and innocent that he began to regret leaving.

"Let's go," Candice said, turning him away.

John could feel Billie's piercing blue eyes on the back of his head, almost making him stop. He turned around, just for a glimpse, just for reassurance that she would be alright, only to see the long trails of tears spilling down her cheeks.

"Daddy," she whispered, reaching for him. "Don't go. Please."

"I'm sorry," he said, more to himself than to her. "I'm sorry."

Even then, with the door closing behind him, and

his wife dragging him away, he wanted to run back to Billie and never leave, whispering his promise in her ear.

John turned, his daughter's cries echoing in his ears. A tear made its way down his cheek, a long line of regret.

That had always been one of the hardest things: making people stay.

Hand in arm, John and Candice stepped out into the night, the darkness embracing them with a sinister hug. The moon peeked through the fog, penetrating the darkness like a searing knife.

John Hagen started the car, pulling away from the woods that bordered their home. The trees looked like giant fingers, reaching for the heavens as if to whisk the stars out of the sky.

He caught one glimpse of his daughter as they barreled away, down the drive that led into downtown Summersville. Billie watched through the open window, hair waving behind her as if to say goodbye.

He reached for his wife's hand, but she snatched it away. Something wasn't right with her; something hadn't been right with Candice in a while.

"You're not yourself," he said.

Candice sighed, her breath fogging up the glass.

"It's nothing," she muttered. Just another lie.

Silence lasted all the way to Summer Café in downtown Summersville. The small diner was known for its laid-back atmosphere and comfort dining, drawing patrons in for an old-time feel. A flashing neon sign suspended by chains banged against the glass window, the metal links clanking in the wind. A bell sounded as the couple stepped through the door, alerting the others to their arrival. The aroma of the Soup of the Day permeated the air—Italian herbs, onion, and freshly minced garlic.

The sizzling of bacon frying on the grill mixed with the tinkling of glass dishes, followed by the slamming kitchen door as waitresses ran back and forth.

Candice led him over to their usual spot in the corner. The oak wood table, covered with a worn checkered cloth, fuzz sprouting from thin holes, was positioned beneath a dim, overhanging lightbulb. It buzzed faintly, glowing a soft, dull yellow.

Tonight, the table hid in the shadows, away from the others whose conversations carried rumors of the latest small-town gossip, echoes of divorce and elections lingering in the small space.

"Somewhere else?"

Candice ignored him, taking a seat. Her eyes wandered throughout the dimly lit room.

John watched her as the waitress hurried over to take their order. Head down, hair sweeping the tops of her eyebrows, Candice picked a new hole in the tablecloth, her sharp fingernails puncturing the covering. She reached for the glass pitcher at the edge of their table, pouring a stream of cold ice tea into her glass. The liquid sloshed over the sides in her shaking hands, staining the cloth.

John started to speak, but the words died before they could slip out. Silence hovered around him, whispering and taunting. Heat rose within his chest. He thought it would drive him mad.

John shifted in his seat, tapped his foot against the

floor, and let out a long sigh.

They left for this?

He imagined poor Billie at home with someone she hardly knew. It was all for nothing.

"Candice, listen, if there's something you're not telling me…"

Her mouth opened, slowly, as if to object. John could almost see the lie forming, growing bigger and bigger, until it eventually tumbled out.

She stared back at him, her face a question.

Spit it out already, his mind screamed. *Please.*

Her blue eyes bore into his, her blond hair seeming to glow in the dark. It was like an older Billie, sitting across from him, a hundred different mysteries all at once.

She leaned forward, tears swimming in the corners of her eyes.

"In three days, I'm going to die."

1

REWIND

Present Day

The unforgiving heat was worse than the thought of the bleached bones.

The sun pounded down on the graveside with a persistent fury. Sweat trickled down Mick's brow, mixing with his tears. The salty brine burned the corners of his mouth. He didn't even try to wipe it away.

Johnson Family Found.

The front page headline rattled around inside Mick's head, whispering the truth in his ears. It never seemed to leave.

He knew anyone that paid attention long enough

could see it, their stares cutting him open like a knife. His thoughts were an open book full of loosely bound pages, falling out at the simplest touch.

The headline came out several days before the funeral, the rumor having finally been addressed. It was yet another shocking turn for Summersville, another grisly find for a town with too many secrets.

It was as if they had all hit 'rewind,' the past springing back.

Clara stood by the open grave, staring down at the casket five feet into the earth. A trace of a tear glistened in the sunlight. Her black dress clung to her skin with sweat, and Mick couldn't help but notice the outline of her bones through the flimsy fabric. Eleven years of captivity, still revealed on her petite frame.

She closed her eyes for one lingering moment, blinking back tears. After all these years, the parents and sibling she'd watched die before her very eyes were finally getting a proper burial.

The skeletal remains were unearthed on Richard Welch's property by the new homeowner. A family of bones, missing for over a decade.

No more secrets. No more lies. It would all soon be over.

The police broke the news to Mick and Clara one evening in their new home. Mick still remembered the captain's words, as dark as the sky outside his window. Just like that, the past they vowed to leave behind had crept back up on them again.

Mick's only gain in his chaotic life was the trust fund left by his great grandfather. The money had given Clara power to regain her independence, impacting her decision to return to where she'd left off all those years ago, before becoming a captive who never saw the light of day. Her decision was a modest house smack-dab in the middle of town. Although inexpensive in real-estate circles, it was rich in her family's legacy. It was her childhood home; a building full of memories, but drained of the Johnson's existence. A place where Clara expected to see their ghosts smiling back at her, welcoming her home.

A precious lie. One she didn't have to think too hard

to believe.

For Mick, it was a new beginning, a chance to have the life and home he had always been deprived of, stolen as a baby and raised by Robert Smith, his family's killer. In the end, the place was just a house; the Johnsons were now stored away beneath the rolling hills of the Chapel Hill Cemetery.

Mick took a deep breath. He could hardly breathe in the stifling heat. All around him, mourners gathered at the site of his family's grave. Death always found a way to lure in a crowd.

Mick didn't know why the news of their return took such a toll on his mind, or even why he found it as shocking as he did. It wasn't like he didn't already know the truth.

Although, it was almost as if the news destroyed the only bit of hope he had left for his family. He'd held onto it ever since his sister returned. If Clara had lived, then who's to say they hadn't?

Closure.

That's what everyone told Mick he had now. That he

could live knowing his family was finally at peace.

Mick didn't have closure. He never would. It wasn't like he could just walk away, turning his back on them forever.

They were family, not just a set of remains that could finally be laid to rest. Not just a set of bones as everyone saw them.

Maybe everyone else could move on, knowing the mystery was solved, that a missing family had been brought home. But Mick just couldn't allow himself to forget.

A hand settled on his shoulder. A woman he'd never seen before stared down at him through a set of wide-rimmed spectacles, flashing a pitied smile.

"Let the wound heal," she whispered. "The more you pick at it, the more it will bleed."

Mick watched something shift behind the woman's eyes—a flash of regret, maybe?—but it faded almost as soon as it had appeared.

She stared at him as if he might break before slinking away down the hill.

Clara's hand slid into his own. She was the only one who understood, more than the crowd gathered around him and the woman who'd spoken just seconds before.

They all thought they were helping, but they only made the pain worse. No one saw Mick and Clara as survivors. They saw them as secrets. And in Clara, they saw a reflection of the past they'd tried to bury, just like they were doing now.

The news of Clara's return hadn't dwindled, it had only grown. The rumors were already beginning to swell. Added in with the finding of her family, the Johnson story had gone national. What with the bank robbery gone wrong and Robert Smith hijacking the Johnson's car while the police were in pursuit, everyone wanted to know more.

News organizations were beginning to reach out to them, vowing to make the truth about the murders and conspiracy in the small, southern town known.

Soon, they would just be the latest gossip passed around the table, thrown out at the viewers from their TV screens; Summersville's sinister history finally revealed.

A family's murder, a fund to kill for, and a missing girl's return equaled a one-way ticket to the spotlight. And in the middle of it all was Mick, who wished it would just go away, to haunt some other family, some other lives who wanted the attention and worshipped the praise.

It wasn't something to be proud of, especially when it had robbed others of their humanity.

Robert Smith, Mr. Welch, Cody Barney, Ms. Crinshaw—a list of names, all co-conspirators in an elaborate plot to take advantage of his family fund. They'd all died because of *him*.

The past kept springing back for Summersville and its people.

And this time, it wouldn't be so easy for them to forget.

2

BURIED TRUTHS

THE BASKETBALL SOARED from Billie's hands, swooping toward the goal. It hit the rim, careening down and bouncing away into the shadows.

An obscenity escaped her mouth. She hurried to finish what she'd started.

The ball rolled into the carport, knocking over a flower pot as it settled to a stop beneath the porch.

Billie got down on all fours, reaching out for the ball. Her fingers were too short to grasp it. She flattened herself against the ground, scooting through the gap under the long, wooden planks.

MCCAID PAUL

This time, she was successful.

With the ball clutched in her hands, she started to back out from under the porch. But a small, silver object hanging on a rusted nail caught her eye.

It was a key.

Her fingers wasted no time in snatching it from its perch. The cool metal seemed to throb beneath them. It dug into her palm as she studied it, her heart drumming in her ears.

This was her dad's…his room…*her mother*…

A shadow fell over her.

"Billie?"

She spun around, hiding the key behind her back.

"Everything alright?" her dad asked, eyebrows raised.

"Yeah, why?"

"I thought I heard—"

"It was just my basketball," Billie confirmed. She gripped the key harder, the metal digging into her skin. "It was an accident."

He nodded, but his face only tightened.

"Just making sure."

His eyes watched her like a hawk, pinning her to the spot.

Eventually, he turned away.

With his back turned, Billie acted. She darted up the steps and slipped into the house, closing the door quietly behind her.

This was her only chance.

Billie's feet pounded the small, spiral staircase as she raced toward the top. She rounded the corner, her eyes focused on the door at the end of the hall.

Not even checking to make sure her dad wasn't following close behind, Billie forced the key into the lock and made her way into his room.

The door let out a loud, agonizing squeal as it swung shut.

Billie crept across the floor, her eyes inspecting the interior.

It was just as she remembered. The same photos of Billie and her dad smiling from the nightstand. A picture of her mother, long, clean blond hair spilling over her shoulders, beaming from a field of dandelions, similar to the one on her dresser. The same pile of wrinkled clothes near the closet.

But this time, Billie knew what she was looking for.

A box sat at the foot of the bed. A newspaper article poked out at the top.

Billie started rummaging through it, shifting through its contents.

The article was the same one she'd stolen from the library seven months prior, back when Billie's best friend, Mick, had first confronted her about the mystery of an abandoned car he'd discovered on Mr. Welch's property, while on a hunting trip with Robert Smith; before all the secrets had upended their life in the worst ways imaginable. Several words and phrases jumped up at her from the paper.

Missing. Possible victim of suicide. Presumed dead.

Billie's mother smiled up at her from the page, her most notable features catching Billie's attention: wavy blond hair, chilling blue eyes, that calm, peaceful smile.

The longer she looked, the longer it took to break away.

Don't get caught in the past.

She set back to work again, her fingers traveling faster than her brain could process. She was about to throw the paper behind her before realizing just what she was grasping in her hands.

It was a medical report, a long list of drugs trekking down the page.

Zoloft.

Lexapro.

Prozac.

All antidepressants.

All prescribed for her mother.

Billie's hands shook. The paper ripped, cutting off some of the names.

The gap ran through a column of bold letters.

Patient: Candice Hagen

Diagnosis: Chronic depression, bipolar disorder

Billie tore the paper in her hands, ripping it to shreds. She threw the medical report beside her, kicking it across the floor.

Her hands froze as she faced the box again.

So many secrets. All locked away.

It took Billie a few moments before she could continue. She took a deep breath, shifting through her mother's past.

An old, busted medicine bottle lay on the cover of a silver journal. Billie snatched the bottle from the pile first. It was one of her mother's prescriptions, several pills laying in fragments on the bottom.

Her eyes were locked on the journal, her fingers reaching out to touch it as the bottle clattered on the floor beside her, falling out of Billie's grasp.

Slowly, she picked up the journal, the weight of its secrets heavy in her hands. She flipped back the cover, spying her mother's words written on the paper. Ink danced across the page, tumbling across the lines like a graceful skater on ice. The words were bold and beautiful, yet black and daunting all the same.

Billie's tears spilled onto her mother's creation, dripping away its beauty, turning it dark, and ugly, as the truth bled through.

Attempt #1: I went to the edge of the abyss today. I almost ended it all, but something held me back. Maybe it was God. Maybe it was love. Maybe it was my daughter. It's dangerous when I get that close. The slightest little nudge would have sent me over. Gone forever.

The journal fell away onto the stained, wooden floor.

Slouched against the wall, her mother's words left Billie broken and confused. Her tears left a puddle on the wood.

There were so many lies. So many secrets. So much *pain*.

Had her mother ended it all in those dark, murky waters? Had she ever looked back on the ones she loved, on everything she might lose?

Why? Why, when Candice had everything? Had she felt she had *nothing*?

No, Billie thought. *My mother wouldn't leave me. Not her.*

Billie didn't believe it. She didn't *want* to believe it. But, yet, she couldn't ignore the evidence lying all around.

What made her mother become the woman she had turned into, right before disappearing? Did she know something that someone didn't want her to? Had someone wanted to keep her quiet?

Or, had she simply given up her will to live?

The thoughts were almost too much to bear. If this was the truth, then all Billie had ever believed about her mother was a lie. Right down to the very end.

Billie stood, packing everything back into the box, leaving no trace behind.

She made her way to the door, stopping to look back for the last time.

Candice Hagen spilled out of the boxes, the cupboards, the drawers. Every secret, and every lie confirmed.

Her mother was everywhere.

Billie closed the door, turned the key in the lock, and walked away, as if she had never been there at all.

3

SECRETS UNREELED

As THE CAMERAS rolled, Clara's instructions flashed through Mick's mind.

"Never look at the camera. Always stare straight ahead. Don't cross your arms or lean back in your chair. Be confident. Don't show them your weakness."

There was a pause, then Clara's final instruction blew hot and sticky against Mick's ear.

"Don't let her win."

Mick snapped back to the present. The reporter flaunted a cold, sneering smile. She didn't have to pretend. Mick could see right through her.

The "special" episode—the woman hadn't been able to hide her sarcasm—would be airing after the nightly news, viewed by Summersville and its other neighboring towns and counties.

The interview took place in their home. The reporter set up in the small, cramped living room, the only available space for her equipment. The place was still in dire need of reconstructing—Clara had swept the old tile floors, rearranged the furnishings, scrubbed the mildew off the walls, knowing it still wasn't enough— but the news station thought the look paired well with the mood they were trying to convey. The living room had fared the best from the rest of the house, pent up and forgotten for almost thirteen years. Maybe the camera could capture it in just the right light; dust hanging in the air, made visible from the beam of sunlight streaming in through the parted, dirty curtains; the wallpaper peeling in a corner of the room, unfurled at the edges.

The reporter's disgust was evident on her scrawny, plastic face the second she walked through their door.

The blond hair hanging over her shoulder reminded Mick of a whip. He could just imagine it tightening around his throat, forcing the answers out of him.

First, she had filmed a segment of herself discussing what the episode would contain. Mick winced, several of the words punching him right in the gut.

"Today, I have the only living survivors of their family's brutal killing, and the only ones who lived to tell the tale."

The sentence was like poison in the young woman's mouth. She showed no remorse, held not even a trace of pity.

It was only news.

Eventually, the reporter moved on to the questions. Mick was first. The interview had begun.

How did you feel about your neighbor, Richard Welch? How often did you and your dad go hunting? Who shot the deer? What did you find in the old beaver pond?

She fired off the questions one right after another. Mick wondered when it would ever end. The woman's words made the painful memories replay themselves in his mind, ugly truths spilling from his mouth every time he spoke.

He started with the hunting trip, Robert Smith shooting the deer, Mick's bold decision to return to Mr. Welch's property to retrieve the animal. Then, he recounted his discovery in the beaver pond: a car, buried under a mound of limbs and tree branches, crumpled and lined with bullet holes, both in and out. A vehicle that belonged to the Johnsons, a missing family who'd disappeared eleven years before.

Billie, his friend on the case they'd mistaken for a game, never realizing just exactly what they were risking; uncovering the truth behind his life in one newspaper headline, the story describing how he once belonged to the Johnsons, that they were *family*. Stolen by their murderer, Robert Smith, for a reason only unlocked by time.

When Mick and Billie had returned to the beaver pond, they were bound in Mr. Welch's home, the stepdad of Robert Smith. Mr. Welch murdered his stepson before he could harm the kids, letting them go for reasons unknown. Five months later, the trial against Welch had come to a close, with no files charged due to a lack of evidence and hearsay.

Of course, all those things came out, eventually. The secrets surrounding Richard Welch's intentions, why he'd saved Mick from the family car when he was an infant.

Mick informed the reporter that, after receiving a letter from his dead sister, he realized that everything he'd been told about Summersville's crimes were a lie. Clara, supposedly a victim in their family's brutal slaying, was very much alive. Held captive in a cell underneath Mr. Welch's barn for the same reason Mick had been saved; a family fund linking the two, a secret that spanned a decade.

Mick tried to speak slow and clear, remaining confident in his answers. He wondered if he displayed enough emotion for the camera, or if he sounded like a tasteless, dull voice.

"How did you feel about the police accidentally killing your mother?"

His sister tensed beside him.

The question had taken both of them off guard.

"I—I mean, I know they didn't mean to do it," Mick said. "It—it's not their fault."

The reporter's eyes seemed to rip him open. It wasn't the answer she was looking for.

Time ticked away. Mick counted down the seconds, waiting for when she chose to strike.

Don't show them your weakness, his sister's voice reminded him.

"What about Billie Hagen, your friend alongside you during this tragedy? Was she a distraction in any way? Did she mislead you in your search for the truth?"

Mick stiffened.

Where were these questions coming from?

A cold sweat broke out on his skin. His face burned. Whatever doubt he once held about his emotional state was gone. Anyone could tell now.

"I don't know what you're getting at," he said, through gritted teeth, "but without Billie, it would have all been useless."

The reporter sneered back at him like a snake, her teeth like fangs.

The interview had taken a turn, and there was no going back.

"Do you know anything about the FBI's recent finding?"

The silence rung in his ears. Mick shook his head, displaying his weakness.

"What if I told you," she said, leaning forward in her chair, "that another set of bullet holes have just been identified in your family's Mustang that do *not* match the ones fired by your stepdad, Robert Smith?"

Her fangs glistened in the pale light. Her smile had never been bigger.

"What would you say then?"

Mick's face turned darker. He gripped the arms of his chair. Before he could speak, his sister intervened.

"You don't have to answer that."

"We're just following procedure," the snake hissed. "You agreed to *all* questions."

Clara stood. "I wouldn't hesitate to drop this. Then

you could go waste someone else's time."

In an attempt to mask her anger, the reporter flashed a calm smile. Underneath, Mick knew she boiled with fury.

"I'm sorry. Let's move on, okay?"

Clara paid the woman no mind, adjusting the microphone clipped to her shirt. She barely had any time before the reporter fired off the next question.

"Did Mr. Welch ever physically harm you? Or, was it different than how we've all imagined it?"

Mick saw the real question shining through, glinting in her cold, wicked eyes: *Did you have feelings for your captor?*

A flash of surprise crossed his sister's face, but only for a second.

Clara drew in for the kill.

Mick could still hear her words.

Don't let her win.

"I was never the girl that gave in. I was never weak. Yet he always found a way of making me feel like I was. I was his victim, and he did things to me no one should ever have to live through. I could never win, but I never gave up. With every punch, with every bruise, he was creating what would eventually destroy him."

Clara took a deep breath, never taking her eyes off the woman sitting in front of her.

"Of course, there will be rumors, there will be secrets, and there most definitely will be lies."

At this, the snake coiled, as if ready to strike.

But Clara wasn't finished.

"And then there's people like *you*, who feed on the gossip, who dive head-first into the lies, ignoring the truth *every single time*."

The serpent stopped, staring at Clara, its mouth dripping with venom.

"I'm as much of a mystery as you want me to be," Clara whispered. "You'll never be able to accept the answers you're given, burying the truth so deep no one will ever be able to find it."

The reporter continued to stare at the woman who had challenged her, no longer hiding her emotions. They melted off her like wax.

"Get out of my house," Clara said.

The reporter wasted no time, quickly gathering her equipment and sprinting to the door. She donned one last smile, looking at Clara as her fingers enclosed around the metal knob. Mick noticed something about her hand, the one clutching a black briefcase stuffed with filming gear—it was shaking.

Mick and Clara watched as she left, her tiny heels clacking against the sidewalk, a curse escaping under her breath as she tripped over the sagging front porch steps. She slammed the car door shut and raced away in the studio van, her skirt ripped and tattered from the tumble down the steps. She'd lost the story everyone would have been talking about, the one that could've promoted her, *famed* her, walking away with nothing but a bruise and a petty excuse the studio would probably believe. She'd tell them how mean the Johnsons were; make them seem like a cunning lot of victims no one should feel sorry for. The truth buried again, all because of someone else's word against another.

Still, her haughty questions lingered behind, echoing in their ears.

Two against one.

"Is it true, Clara?" Mick's voice trembled. "Did the FBI find more bullet holes?"

Clara blinked. Mick thought tears formed there, in the corner of her eyes, but she turned away before he could be sure. She left him standing alone, the questions weighing him down. It was then that Mick realized he had been wrong.

Clara was still being held captive. And this time, there was no escape.

4

SHALLOW WATERS

THEY DEPARTED AT sunrise.

After a quick lie to his sister, Mick left to meet up with Billie, joining his friend in her search for answers. They headed toward Springs Bridge, merging the space between Summersville and White Springs.

Tombstones popped up on their left, dotting the hills that seemed to rise and swell behind the longstanding Baptist church. If Mick allowed himself to look long enough, his mind would replay the events of the shooting there, two months ago, that had left him in an open grave and his sister with a gunshot wound.

Upon his return, he and Billie found the only link to Clara and the only evidence of her possible killer: a single shell-casing. It had been missed in the police's investigation, left for Mick, who later identified its owner. It belonged to the librarian, also known as Ms. Claudia, a woman who had aided them along in their investigations; one who'd provided them with many of the town's forgotten secrets. A person Mick had grown to trust.

Now, suffering from a mild form of amnesia, Ms. Claudia was being kept in a local nursing facility. For the rest of her days, she would live with the disorder, rotting away with her secrets.

Mick hadn't been to the library since.

Black-and-white dairy cows grazed in their pastures, raising their heads as they passed. They continued on, heading deeper into the country, their bikes rolling along on the pavement.

A blanket of silence draped over the two. They enjoyed the tranquility of the rural area as they soaked in the beauty of the early morning.

The sun rose amidst the vivid hues that faded with the clouds. Shades of yellow, orange, and red poured throughout the countryside, giving the trees golden crowns, the grass a glistening, glowing dew, and the water a mirror of the sky.

It wasn't long before the silence was broken, and his earlier thoughts came springing back.

"How was the interview?" Billie asked.

Mick groaned. He explained every detail of it, to the reporter's insolence, her personal, relentless questions they couldn't avoid, and his sister's bold decision to cancel the interview.

"Don't blame her," Billie said. "But Mick, really? Have I taught you nothing? You gotta show em' who's boss. Put that finger up for the camera, nice and square. Viewers like some action."

"If only I was like you," Mick smirked, not even in the least surprised at Billie's brashness.

"People only care about what sells. If it will benefit them, then they're all for it. Welcome to the world of crooks."

"Tell me about it," Mick mumbled. His friend—if they considered themselves that anymore—had a point. In the reporter's mind, it was only news, only an hour of soundbites that could enhance a career. Who cared about professionalism when it could give them a little dose of fame?

The topic shifted to the reporter's revelation—the FBI's newest finding.

"More bullet holes? Are you sure? If they weren't from your stepdad..." Billie trailed off. Mick could almost see the wheels turning in her head.

"It was from the police, when they accidentally killed my mother. They tried to cover it up, even forget about it, but the FBI has other intentions. They might reopen a whole new case against the police, making sure justice is served."

"What did Clara say?"

"She wants me to let it go. She doesn't want to be thrown back into it all again. Clara knows it wasn't the police's fault...they were only trying to stop the robber. But it still feels so wrong, and I know she feels it, too.

How can we trust the ones who killed a member of our family? Isn't that just going against what they practice?"

"It was a mistake, Mick."

"But was it?"

Billie slowed. She shook her head.

"You're telling yourself a lie. Stop burying the truth."

They continued on their way again, the silence settling back over them.

Stop burying the truth.

Isn't that what Clara said the reporter was doing? Here he was now, just as guilty. Morphing into the snake he hoped to never become.

. . . .

With the colors of the sky now just a mere blemish on the clouds, the beauty of the sunrise was long gone, replaced with the pulsating glow of the sun. The area around them rose and fell in shadow, like a yellow bruise on pale skin.

It wasn't long before the bridge came into view, the trees opening up to reveal the long-awaited answers from Billie's mother's past. But when they drew closer, their previous notions of the bridge's appearance slipped away and drowned.

The place was unlike anything Billie imagined. Instead of a high structure rising above a mile long ravine as she had dreamed of it being, the bridge was barely tall enough for shelter underneath. Where she expected the water to be dangerous and threatening, now it transformed into a small creek, a mere tributary.

The bridge was just wide enough for two cars to cross, but not one had passed since they'd arrived.

Billie stared in shock at the sight before her. Springs Bridge wasn't some towering structure rising over a gorge. Instead, it was a little country bridge with shallow waters. A place where suicide seemed unimaginable.

Candice Hagen supposedly jumped to her death from Springs Bridge—which began to seem even more plausible after Billie's recent findings—and a local fisherman supported the claim.

But that was five years ago. And now, the secrets were beginning to surface.

Staring out at the water, Billie realized that had never

been the truth at all. Just a lie, one the town had done their best to believe. Turning the truth into a secret they had done their best to forget.

"Here's what we know," Billie said, counting off everything on her fingers. "My mother disappeared sometime between the night and morning of October 12th. She failed to report to her shift at the nursing center, and later her car and purse were found abandoned here. The same day, a local fisherman saw a person jump into these waters."

"It doesn't add up," Mick said, the truth glinting in his eyes. He stared out at the rippling water, too shallow to drown a body.

"Now you see, don't you? If my mother wanted to kill herself, why here? Why not another bridge with a higher elevation and deeper waters? If she was so committed, why did she rule out the most common place in town?"

"The Dead Forest," Mick whispered.

"I don't think we're looking for a suicide here. Much less a murder. All this time, this place has been a ploy. A distraction. We've just been chasing a ghost."

Billie leaned against Mick, the answers seeming to weigh her down. "It's been five years, and I've never once been here. This place has been a part of my life ever since my mother vanished, and not once have I had the guts enough to confront the truth. Now, I realize why. I was afraid of what I might find."

"You've been believing a lie," Mick said. "Don't feel guilty. The town has only made it worse."

Billie's words flashed across her mind.

Stop burying the truth.

"If I had just come sooner," Billie whispered. "Maybe then I would have already known. I've only wasted time, and now it may be too late."

As obvious as it all seemed, other questions pressed in on her. If suicide wasn't possible here, then why was her mother's car left behind? What about the person the fisherman claimed to have seen jump?

"Then what about her car and purse?" Mick asked, stealing her thoughts. "And the fisherman, could he have been lying?"

"Unless her body was dumped here and the fisherman saw her killer throw her from the bridge. That explains the car and purse. It was staged to make it look like she killed herself, when it was always the other way around."

"Maybe...but how wouldn't the fisherman have seen who it was?"

Mick paused.

"Maybe we're overthinking it. Maybe the water used to be deeper."

Billie knew it was a stretch, the *whole thing* felt like a stretch. Coming here had only posed more questions, ones they may never get the answers to. Candice Hagen's disappearance was a mystery, but so was Candice Hagen herself.

"If the fisherman saw my mother's killer, then maybe he was forced to keep the secret. He might have been blackmailed, which is why he lied..." She trailed off, before adding, "Unless he did it himself."

Whether in a fit of rage, or as an intent to soothe his bloodlust, a complete stranger could've ended her mother. If it was a stranger at all.

Where are you, Mom? Billie thought. *Where are you?*

If she looked long enough, she could almost make out her mother smiling up at her from the creek. Even though it wasn't deep enough for a body, her mother made the truth seem like a lie, slipping away beneath the water before Billie could say goodbye.

She leaned further into Mick as her vision faded, resting her head in the crevice of his shoulder. Even with all that had happened, she felt safe when she was with him, like nothing could harm them when they were together.

But Billie knew she was wrong.

Danger seemed to follow in Mick's footsteps.

Apart, they were safe. Together, they were dangerous.

Where would this lead? She almost didn't want to find out...

Either way, now that the line had been crossed, there was no going back.

She still heard Mick's words in her mind. *Something more. Something different.*

Their promise to each other. One they would never tell her father. One they were struggling to keep.

They hadn't mentioned it since that day a month ago, and Billie wondered if it meant anything anymore. Like her mother, perhaps it, too, had drifted away.

They stared out at the water, lost in their own thoughts. From killers, to mothers, to lies, to buried truths.

"You think it was your Uncle David, don't you?" Mick asked.

Billie's lips parted. The name itself made her insides twist into a tight knot.

The last time she'd heard his name, it was to do with the death threats he'd sent her mother before she disappeared. Creeping into her dad's room, uncovering the letter stored away in his desk drawer, a vital secret he'd never bothered to tell her.

So many secrets she'd never been told, promised to be for her safety. Nothing else.

But the more she thought about it all—the death threats, the secrets locked away in her dad's room—the more confused she became, questions chasing after questions through her muddied mind.

Billie put a hand to her head, squeezing her eyes shut. She didn't think she breathed at all.

"It could have been any one of them."

5
PHOBIA

WITH THE LEADS from her mother's case seeming more and more like dead ends as the days faded into another, Billie no longer knew where to look. She was on the verge of giving up when the answer came to her in the form of a shrunken, scraggly old man who whispered his sermons underneath his breath like a second language.

Mr. Abram, the youth pastor at the venerable Chapel Hill Baptist Church, usually made Billie want to fall asleep during his hour-long messages, but on this particular occasion, she was listening.

The rather ancient, diminutive man had just announced his future ideas for the youth group when he dismissed their usual Wednesday afternoon with a change of plans.

"Reckon you're all expectin' my lesson any moment now," he said in his typical southern drawl, "but I don't always stick to the book. Tonight we're takin' a special trip. I won't tell you where…you'll have to find out for yourself."

They boarded the bus, leaving behind the red velvet pews and haunting melodies from the worship choir that rang pure with conviction. Billie sat beside Mick, breaking the prehistoric bus rule that separated the boys from the girls. Mr. Abram would never know; his eyesight was as foggy as a pair of glasses in the middle of a rainstorm.

They sped past the cemetery, the headstones like tangled teeth, protruding every which way. The Chapel Hill Baptist Church had the oldest graves from the first settlers, the graveyard serving as a footprint, a clue in time to its legacy. There were even rumors that the first tomb was buried somewhere under the building.

Billie had no idea what awaited her at Mr. Abram's planned destination; it wasn't like him to change things up a bit. She could only hope that his old age hadn't finally gotten the better of him.

Minutes later the bus pulled into a large front lot, coming to a stop near the glass doors that marked the entrance.

"What do y'all think?" the old youth pastor inquired with a wide, nearly toothless grin.

Billie stared at the drab walls and stained brick, a few flowers dotting the campus in an attempt to make the place seem more welcoming. "A nursing home?" she exclaimed, the first one to speak.

All eyes were pinned on Mr. Abram. A phlegmy cough rattled somewhere deep inside his throat, resonating into a maniacal laugh.

Thoughts flooded Billie's mind about her youth leader's sanity. Had Mr. Abram finally given up? Was now the time for his students to bid him his final farewell?

Images came to her, ones of wrinkled forms in over-sized gowns, skin barely covering their bones; of long, pointy fingers reaching out to pull her into their rooms, watching her through bloodshot eyes as they licked their cracked lips. Billie searched for a way out.

"We're goin' in, whether y'all like it or not. We'll divide in our teams and meet up in the lobby in an hour. Talk to as many folks as you can, and remember to pray with 'em. They'll get more out of this than y'all will."

With that, Mr. Abram concluded his pep talk, ushering them out.

Billie groaned as she grudgingly followed; she was the last one from the bus. Mick dragged her along, keeping a step behind the crowd of students.

"What's wrong with you?"

"I...can't...do...it," Billie sputtered, her breath shaking in between every word. "Old people...." She shook her head. "Gerontophobia. It's a real thing. Look it up."

"Mr. Abram doesn't seem to bother you. So why do

—"

"Forget it, Mick!" she shouted, attracting several eyes from the youth group. Mr. Abram didn't seem to notice. "I can't stand the thought of it...the thought of *them*..."

"What? Growing old? It's a real thing," Mick mocked. "Look it up."

Billie rolled her eyes. "It sounds better when I say it."

The glass doors opened and a gust of cold air rushed out to meet them. A shiver ran up Billie's spine, stopping at the nape of her neck. She was pretty sure it wasn't just because of the temperature.

Against her objections, Mick pushed her inside. She wrapped around him, begging for anything to hold onto.

An oppressive odor of stale urine mixed with cleaning chemicals pressed on Billie's senses, making her gag.

She studied the building's wide hallways and dim lighting. The oyster-shell colored tile floor appeared like it had received a lot of traffic over the years. The only thing missing was the maintenance worker walking behind the huge floor buffing machine, visible within almost every institution ever built.

They were just rounding the corner when Billie stopped dead in her tracks. She stared straight ahead, eyes locked on the door in front of them.

"Are you okay?" Mick asked as Billie let him go.

She lifted a shaking finger to the silver nameplate mounted on the wood.

"McLain," she muttered. "I know that name."

Her body stiffened, eyes narrowing to mere slits.

"Billie?"

"It's him, Mick."

"Who?"

She sucked in a long breath. Her eyes met his. "The fisherman."

6

AN UNWILLING WITNESS

BILLIE TURNED ON her heel, sprinting away down the hall.

"Billie!" Mick called, but his friend showed no signs of stopping. She slipped out of sight, her blond hair trailing behind as she disappeared around the corner.

Mick raced after her, his feet pounding on the tile. He finally spotted Billie at the end of the hall, her hands propped on the desk of a nurse's station.

Just as Mick came to a halt beside her, Billie flashed a fake smile at the desk attendant. The manipulator was at work.

"Hi, so sorry to bother you! I'm looking for one of my relatives and I was hoping you could help me find him?"

The nurse stared down at Billie through her wide-rimmed glasses. A smile widened across her lips.

"Sure, honey! Can you give me his name?"

"Mr. McLain."

Mick emitted a small gasp. The nurse didn't seem to notice.

"I'm his niece and I haven't seen him in a while."

Out of the corner of her eye, Billie gave a small wink. Mick's mouth dropped in surprise, surprised at how far Billie was willing to take her deception.

The woman swooned. "Right this way."

Billie took a step forward, but Mick pulled her back.

"Billie—"

"I know what I'm doing," she whispered, strutting farther ahead of him, an innocent smile stretching across her face. "Don't ruin it now."

Her lies had given her a newfound boldness, making it appear as if she never had a phobia of the place. As if that, too, was only a lie. Mick had seen Billie pull it off before, yet if she wasn't careful, she might slip under the weight of her fabrications.

The nurse came to a halt outside the door. She bent down to Billie's height, noticing Mick over Billie's shoulder for the first time.

She smiled. "Is this your boy—"

"He's my friend," Billie said, her face flushing bright red. "Now, may I see my uncle?"

"Listen, honey, you might not know, but Mr. McLain hasn't been doing well lately. He might not remember you, so don't be discouraged. He's like this with all of our residents and staff."

"Why is that?" Billie asked.

The woman hesitated. "He has Alzheimer's."

Billie lowered her gaze to the floor. "Okay," she whispered sadly, but Mick could see a glint of mischief in her eyes. It was all working in her favor.

Mick's heart sank. The man's condition gave her an excuse. He needed to put a stop to this before things got out of hand; before Mr. Abram found out. She had already taken things too far.

Mick opened his mouth to speak, but it was too late.

She slipped inside behind the nurse, crossing the threshold to his room. "Mr. McLain, your niece is here to see you."

The lump in the bedsheets stirred. A hairy, wrinkled hand reached out to pull the sheets down from underneath his chin.

He stared out at them through small slits. A grimace pulled on his face.

"Thank you, miss," Billie said to the nurse. "I've got it from here."

The woman nodded, softly closing the door behind her.

Billie took a step forward. Mick stood frozen in place.

"Mr. McLain?" she whispered. "It's me…Billie. Your niece."

The man's snarl faded. His cracked lips turned upward in a smile.

"Billie…I like that name."

His words came out scratchy and slow, as if it required much effort to speak. His hair hung in wisps, like long lines of fishing wire. They brushed his tan skin, holding proof of too many hours spent under the sun.

"How are you?" Billie asked.

The calm before the storm, Mick thought.

Mr. McLain sighed. "These nurses treat me like nothin'. I just wanna go home. My wife oughta already have the fire goin'."

Mick felt a tinge of pity. He wanted to get Billie out of here. She was taking advantage of an old man, one who couldn't even remember.

"Mr. McLain," Billie whispered. She let the silence stretch on for what felt like minutes. "What did you see five years ago on the morning of October 12th?"

The man's lips parted. He sucked in a long breath.

"I...I can't remember."

"Mr. McLain."

Her words were soft. Delicate. "Springs Bridge... Candice Hagen..."

The man struggled to respond. He seemed agitated,

distraught.

Mick wanted to believe him, but there was something there, something in the way his face darkened when Billie mentioned Candice Hagen, something in the way his eyes flashed when he heard the date.

He was caught in Billie's web, and she knew it.

"Who else did you see? Who else was with you on that bridge?"

McLain's head wobbled on his shoulders, his wrinkled hands clenching into fists.

Billie leaned closer. "Or did you do it yourself?"

The man rose. He pounded the bedsheets, cursing like a sailor. He stared Billie dead in the eye, pointing his finger in her face.

Billie didn't budge, even with the spit trickling down her cheek and the man's hateful words. Instead, she took another step forward.

"You could have stopped her," she whispered. "You could have saved her."

Mr. McLain froze. He plopped back on the bed,

staring off at nothing. If Mick knew better, he was caught in a memory.

"She didn't need saving," he said, turning to look at her. "Not from me. Only herself."

Billie stared at the man, as if she were deciding whether his answer was enough.

"Thanks, Mr. McLain."

She turned away. Mick followed her out the door, leaving behind their witness.

The nurse met them in the hall, her face wide with concern. "I thought I could get there in time...I could hear him all the way down the hall."

"It's fine," Billie said like a sad, small little girl. "I didn't realize how bad he'd become."

The woman patted her on the back, believing Billie's lie...if it even was a lie at all. Mick couldn't help but wonder. She'd wanted answers, only to get a torrent of obscenities. They'd gotten nowhere.

When the nurse was sure Billie would be alright, she left them alone, her feet clicking along against the tile floor, back to the desk at her station.

"What were you thinking?" Mick exclaimed through gritted teeth. "If you want to do this, I'm done."

Mick turned his back on her, expecting a hand to reach out and stop him; a voice to admit its mistake.

But she let him go.

Mick walked away, lost in his fury. He wandered around in a daze, his mind in a constant fog. All he could think about was Billie…how he wondered if he ever knew her…if she was just using him too, just like the fisherman. Of all the years they'd been friends, of all the secrets they shared, of all the promises they made, Mick never knew just what she might be capable of.

"Sir?" a weak voice called from behind.

Mick kept going. He pretended he hadn't heard, continuing on in his daze, consumed by his thoughts.

It wasn't until he made it to the end of the hall that the voice returned. "Sir? Can you take me to my room?"

Mick halted. His thoughts slipped away. His breath hitched in his throat. He slowly turned.

He recognized that voice. He would know it anywhere.

Mick faced the woman, staring down into the eyes of his enemy; of someone he'd once thought a friend.

There, sitting in her wheelchair, that distinct question mark perched between her eyebrows, was Ms. Claudia.

7

AID TO THE ENEMY

Mick was trapped.

He stood frozen in terror, his legs refusing to move, refusing to run away.

It was just the two of them. Alone. Again.

Ms. Claudia could do anything she wanted. This time, there was nothing he could use to stop her.

"Sir?" The question came out like a command.

Mick drew a breath.

She can't remember. She means me no harm.

Seconds ago, his heart pounded like a jackhammer, but now it was a steady pace against his ribs. His adrenaline lessened. He managed a step forward.

"Can you take me to my room, dear?" she asked again. "For the life of me, I can't recall where it is."

Mick gripped the handles of her wheelchair, as multiple images came rushing back.

Her fingernails, scratching his face. The bookshelf, plummeting through the air. Her hand, sticking out from underneath the wreckage.

Limp.

Lifeless.

Broken.

But not anymore.

They strolled across the floor, shrunken figures and grinning skeletons watching as they passed. Mick searched for her name among the silver nameplates mounted on the doors.

She began to hum. It was soft, subtle, almost a whisper. Mick couldn't place the tune, though he knew he'd heard it before.

The hum seemed to increase in volume. He tried to block it from his mind, but it only grew louder.

The clicks of the wheels on the tile floor was like a beat to her song. Mick shook his head in an effort to drive the noises out. They formed a haunting melody, throbbing in his skull. He begged for it to stop.

It's a game, Mick thought. Her *game.*

"Sir?"

She's faking. She's toying with me. She knows. She knows who I am.

"Sir?" Louder this time.

He breathed heavily, waiting for Ms. Claudia to make her move, waiting for what he deserved.

That day in her home, when he'd found Clara tied up and unconscious in Ms. Claudia's tub, Mick had wanted nothing more than to have justice, fueled by fear that he couldn't control. She'd chased him, tried to kill him even, and he'd acted on impulse, sending her here, a fate worse than death. No memory, no recollection. Constantly lost, constantly confused.

But what else could he have done? Why did he feel so guilty, when he was only trying to protect himself?

"I'm sorry," he whispered, remembering the sound of

her bones cracking underneath the weight of the shelf, an ugly scream forcing its way out of her small body at the last second. "I never meant it, *not any* of it."

Ms. Claudia's face wrinkled in confusion. "Sorry for what, dear?"

I'm crazy, Mick thought, a moment later. *She really can't remember.*

He put a hand to his spinning head. He thought he could still hear her hum, trapped somewhere deep within him.

What's wrong with me?

"It's nothing," Mick said. "I thought you were someone else."

He resumed his stroll down the long hallway. It seemed to stretch for miles.

Names surrounded them from every side, but none of them were hers.

After a while, Mick thought about giving up, leaving her to find it on her own, away from his enemy who might still remember his intentions.

Yet there it was, mounted on the wood.

Welch.

Just a glimpse of it brought back what Mick had so desperately tried to forget. It was a name riddled with misfortune, one that unlocked the secrets from his painful past.

The gunshot. Mr. Welch's body. His blood staining the leaves.

Fear twisted in Mick's gut. The memories were razor-sharp.

Fog, swirling through dead trees. Ms. Crinshaw's final cries as she drowned. Cody Barney lunging to sink his teeth into him.

"Is everything alright, dear?" Ms. Claudia stared up at him through worried eyes.

Her words cut through the pain, the images slipping away from where they'd come. Mick uttered a soft apology.

Her room was the last one along the hall. His hand reached out for the knob.

*No...*something wasn't right here. His hand trembled, dropping from the metal.

There was a lock on the door. One long, thick bolt. But it wasn't on the inside.

A shiver rippled through him like the cold, rippling waters off Springs Bridge. Bile rose in his throat.

How had she escaped? And why was she here now, asking him for help?

"Did—did someone let you out?" Mick shuddered as his eyes met her glassy stare. It was like she was looking right through him.

"I'm sorry. I don't think I understand—"

But Mick did. The answer came to him as his fingers closed around the icy metal. He knew why she was here. Maybe she did, too.

After the incident in Ms. Claudia's library, and after Ginger, the investigator on the case, saved Mick and Clara from the house, the medical team accepted the obvious: Ms. Claudia wouldn't ever recover, mentally or physically, given the blow to her head that resulted in amnesia.

Of course, given her state, she no longer posed a threat. But it appeared the facility wasn't taking any chances.

Someone had let Ms. Claudia out. Maybe a curious teenager who didn't know what they were doing, or a sympathetic staff member that thought she just needed some exercise.

Or, maybe, she had done it. Maybe, for the first time since the incident, she got a flash of a memory and let herself out somehow.

Maybe Ms. Claudia had always been looking for him.

Mick turned. She was humming again, smiling widely from her wheelchair. Her feet bounced up and down. She didn't seem to realize he was there anymore.

Mick gripped the handles and wheeled her into her room. He would drop her off and leave before she ever noticed; locking her in like she deserved to be. Rotting away with the flashes of memories, multiple personalities, and secrets she would always live with, contained behind the infamous name mounted outside the door.

Darkness filtered out into the hall from the dim

room. Shadows blanketed the space, a curtain of inky darkness draped over the small chamber. His fingers searched for the light switch.

The light flickered for several seconds before finding a place where it seemed comfortable. Newspapers littered the floor. Piles of books rested on the windowsill, one laying half-open on the pillow in her bed. The air smelled offensive and stale.

"Thank you," she said, as he wheeled her to a stop. He was turning to leave when he heard it.

His name. Coming from her mouth.

"Mick," she whispered, the word a piercing wound, searing and sharp. He slowly turned.

Mick saw it in her eyes, a flash of remembrance.

But then it was gone.

. . . .

The house was centered between whitewashed homes and neatly clipped hedges, in a neighborhood where families sat under the stars, grilled in their backyards, and packed memories within a 1,500 square foot modest home. Twelve years before, one particular family had done the same. Their property used to match the others, changing with the holidays and the adorned styles popular with each passing year.

Now, it was the place everyone tried not to see. They couldn't be reminded of the peaceful Johnsons whose kids used to play with their own, or who laughed in their very home on the eve of every New Year.

The front porch sagged, the barn in the back had collapsed in on itself, and the paint was chipped away in places, giving it a dark, rundown look due to the lack of decoration and abundance of mildew. The yard was overtaken by trees, ranging from sweet gum to oak.

Passersby would still catch a glimpse every now and then, claiming to have seen a face at the window, or a dull light in a back room. Even with the news of their deaths, they all still held a desire in their heart to see them walk out of the gloom and back into their lives again; into the home that was left to rot and decay in the time of their absence. No one wanted to believe that a normal, everyday family could be murdered in a town where nothing was supposed to go wrong.

The night tugged on the sun, pulling it farther away beneath the rolling hills. Mick trudged up the sagging porch and crumbling stone steps. The floorboards creaked with every step, shifting under his weight.

Clara stood in the doorway.

"How was church?"

"Typical Wednesday night."

He brushed past her. He hoped she wouldn't recognize his lie.

His sister stared a second too long, her pale face wrinkling in confusion. "What's wrong?"

"Nothing."

She put a trembling hand on his shoulder. "It's good to be home, isn't it?"

Home.

"Yeah, it is."

She nodded, her green eyes glowing in the light from the kitchen. Her face was fuller, no longer displaying any signs of malnutrition or neglect.

Mick remembered a previous night when he'd slipped into the kitchen for a glass of water. His sister had been sitting by the window, staring out into the night, her pale skin almost ghastly under the light of the moon.

The lack of sunlight in the cell left her with a permanent stain; it was the only proof of her captivity.

He would never understand what she went through in that cell, what horrors she encountered, what long nights she screamed until she lost her voice. For safety. For rescue. For her brother.

And in return, all she got was Mr. Welch, an old, miserable man who had no intention of ever letting her go. One whose last image of his captive was the flash from the end of the gun, and her figure fading into the darkness. Running back to her past, a place just as dangerous as the one she left behind.

"Clara," Mick whispered, his eyes lost in the fire blazing in the hearth. "What do you know about Candice Hagen?"

The grip on his shoulder tightened. His sister let out a painful sigh. "Don't do this to me."

"I just want an answer. If you know something that

can help, then why can't you tell?"

"You don't know me."

She turned away, but Mick didn't notice; he still stared aimlessly into the fire, fixated on the flames.

Here he was, telling Billie to move on, when he couldn't even do it himself. He wished he could just leave it alone, but he knew where to find answers. They lurked within his very home. Bearing a face of his sister, but underneath a stranger, keeping the secrets as her own.

Candice Hagen—Mick realized—never died; she was the beating heart in his sister's soul. Throbbing, pulsing within her, the framework that held Clara together. A secret locked in a cage, as bloody and alive as an internal organ.

"All I wanted to do was get away," she said from the window behind him. The fire danced on her skin, sparkling in her eyes. "Have a fresh start. Begin a life with the only person I had left." She met his gaze, her face seeming to sag. "But all you want to do is keep bringing it back. The past is the past. Let it go. It's not worth it. It's not safe."

"Why?" His voice cut into her words, beating them down. He needed her to break. He needed her to confess.

She swallowed. "Some people are only out to protect themselves."

Mick stared at his sister. She was suddenly more interesting than the blazing fire.

He knew he was hurting her; knew he was hurting them both. His sister would never be the same, but he could at least try not to make it worse.

Once he got a clue, he couldn't stop. It was an addiction. Something he craved.

Ever since learning the truth about his own life, he had desired to feel that power again. It was what calmed his doubt and fear, giving him the strength in Ms. Claudia's house to live; the thing that saved him from the hands of his enemies in the forest. What almost every time seemed to push him to the brink of insanity. What almost every time seemed to lead to his end.

If there was one thing he'd learned since finding his

family's car in that old beaver pond, it was that the truth can be a very powerful thing.

And the past—it was here now. It was in the ghosts between the walls, in the memories burning like a constant fire. To Clara, it was in the stories unfolding in every room, in the cracks between the floorboards, and in the window where her mother used to comb her hair. If they continued to live here, if his sister continued to dwell in the past, her mind would lose hold of the things around her, showing her images and faces that had already passed; sending herself and her secrets to a place where Mick might not ever be able to get her back.

"I'm finally here. Back to where I used to be. With the ones that loved me more than anything. Yet why do they feel so far away?"

"They're gone, Clara. This place doesn't hold any evidence of them anymore."

"But it should!" She turned to face him, tears glimmering in her eyes.

"They're not coming back." He didn't realize he was

standing until her hand reached out for his. "What was it you said? The past is the past. Let it go. You've been holding onto it this entire time."

"I know…I'm sorry…"

"But you have me. Isn't that what you always wanted?"

The sobs seemed to rip her open, coming out of her like violent, dry heaves. It was an ugly, painful sound.

Mick did the only thing he knew to do—he wrapped his arms around her, knowing that if he let her go, she might break into a million pieces on the floor.

8

COME FIND ME

MISSING. PRESUMED DEAD. Possible victim of suicide.

Billie took a deep breath. She closed her eyes.

Springs Bridge. The fisherman. The death threats. Uncle David's claims.

Clara. The stranger at her door, whispering a secret she'd kept for years as Mr. Welch's captive.

I know something about your mother.

So many clues. So many secrets.

Billie stared up at the ceiling in the darkness of her room. Her breaths were calm despite her growing apprehension.

Her mother was gone. Forgotten. Just a ghost everyone tried their best not to see.

Her mother.

The emotions swelled in Billie's throat. She struggled to breathe.

How could it be that the woman who used to tuck her in at night, sing her lullabies, and comb her hair was dead? How could it be that the town had forgotten her —that her own daughter had forgotten her?

She'd just been trying to move on, leaving the mother she once knew in the past. Leaving her memory to rest, so she didn't have to remember. Becoming so caught up in one part of her mother's life and confusing it for the whole.

Billie remembered the way her mother used to smile. The nights she slept with her when her dad wasn't home; their trips to the field of dandelions behind their house. She'd always felt so safe back then. Secure. Knowing that nothing could happen to them. Not her. Not Candice.

Until the day her mother didn't come home. Until the day she waited all night for her mother to come tuck her in.

"Goodnight, my dandelion," she used to whisper, before she turned the light out and only darkness remained. Those were the last words she'd ever heard her mother say.

The thoughts slipped from Billie's mind when she heard the creak on the stairs. She wrapped up in her bedsheets and closed her eyes as the door opened. Her dad peered out at her through the large crack, silently closing her bedroom door. His footsteps pattered down the stairs again. A door slammed shut somewhere in the back of the house.

No "goodnight." Only a glimpse. For him, it was enough.

That's what made fathers different from mothers, Billie had come to understand. Mothers displayed affection a father could only begin to express in words. Mothers told stories and held their child close. They weren't supposed to leave. They weren't supposed to take their life to lessen their pain. They were supposed to live with it, not drown in it.

"Mama," Billie whispered, like the word itself could bring her back. She should have learned by now not to believe in miracles. The dead didn't return. Dead was dead. That was it.

But now, she wasn't so sure.

Her mother was here. She could feel it.

Whether in a dream, or just the product of a loss of sleep, she watched the door creak open to reveal a slender figure standing in the doorway.

Her mother.

"Goodnight, my dandelion," she said, but this time, her voice was all wrong. It faltered, dropping when it was supposed to rise.

"Come find me," she muttered, her footsteps racing down the stairs like a drawn out whisper. Billie followed, her mind not in pace with her legs.

Her mother was a speck among the trees, running faster and faster still; a ghost sailing in the night, her hair billowing and gleaming in the frozen, frost-filled air.

Come find me.

The words lurked behind every tree, hidden from the light. A tremor in the silent night.

Branches clawed Billie's skin, seeming to rip her alive. Roots sent her sprawling on the forest floor.

Suddenly, the trees opened to reveal Springs Bridge. Billie tried to run, but the branches kept reaching out to grab her, holding her back.

Her mother was too far ahead; she couldn't stop her. Not this time.

Her name lodged in Billie's throat as she jumped over the side, careening down to the murky depths. She waited for the final scream sinking away beneath the surface, the only thing left.

Billie slipped out of the branches grasp, her feet meshing with the soil, pushing through the fear that threatened to swallow her whole.

She willed a peek over the side. Staring down at the sparkling, glistening creek, Billie expected to find a body floating downstream.

But her mother wasn't there. It was almost as if she never *was*.

She'd watched her mother jump...seen it with her own two eyes.

So why hadn't there even been a splash?

9
DECEPTION

THE TRAILER WAS a rundown, ramshackle place on the outskirts of town. Billie dropped her bicycle in the overgrown grass of her uncle's front yard, wading in the weeds to the door.

The screen creaked open slightly, revealing two bloodshot eyes that peered out at her. A hand fumbled for the knob.

Uncle David stood in the doorway, a beer bottle clasped in hand. He spat in the dead plant at his feet, wiping his mouth with his sleeve. His lips twitched with a crazy smile.

"You know you're not supposed to be here."

"I just want to talk."

He snorted and held the door open, allowing her inside.

Beer bottles were strewn across the floor. A half-eaten can of beans had attracted a swarm of flies, and the furniture was worn and sagging. Billie sidestepped to avoid the glass, but to no avail, as it crunched beneath her feet.

The door shut behind them. Billie's fingers brushed the pocket knife in her jean pocket. She knew her uncle and his alcoholic ways. He wasn't someone she could trust. No, he was downright unpredictable.

He motioned for her to have a seat.

She grudgingly complied. The couch was covered with a sheet, as well as his recliner. It was obvious he was trying to cover up the stains and cigarette burns.

Billie sat on the end, opposite her uncle, who sprawled back in his recliner.

"Whadda ya' want?" he slurred.

"I know what you did."

Her uncle smiled, taking a long sip from his bottle. "And what may that be?"

"The threats. To my mother."

The bottle lowered. His smile faded. "Your daddy tell you that?"

"What if *you* did?" Billie prodded. "You're too drunk half the time to notice."

He shook his head. "You've lost it, princess. I ain't that dumb."

Billie recalled the night he'd let several sentences slip, making her question everything she knew about her mother's disappearance.

Have you ever thought that your daddy might have pushed your momma off the bridge? He's not the man you think he is. Be careful.

It was the first clue she ever received regarding her mother. Yet both Billie and her uncle knew the answer. It wasn't a clue, it was a half-baked lie. Her dad had nothing to do with pushing his wife from a bridge.

"Why did you do it?" Billie asked, leaning closer. "You're her brother. Didn't you love her?"

He snarled, revealing snuff-stained teeth. "You're getting in over your head. You better quit while you can, before you end up like *her*."

"Candice. Her name is Candice."

He drained the last of the drink, a frothy mess in the bottom of the bottle. "I suppose it is."

"Tell me why, David," she whispered. "It was just a prank, right? There's no harm in that."

The corners of his lips twitched. He knew he was being played.

"You wouldn't understand."

"That's right. I'm not a drunk like you."

Her uncle tightened his grip around the bottle. His knuckles were white.

Billie slowly undid the knife in her pocket. Any sudden moves, and she wouldn't hesitate to strike.

"You think I chose this?" he asked. "That I wanted this?"

He slammed the bottle against the wall. Billie jumped as it shattered into a thousand shards, stabbing the stained carpet. His head was in his hands. His body shook.

"Uncle David, I'm sorry…"

But he wasn't crying. He was *laughing*. Echoes of rage replaced with a bellowing fit of amusement, manic and loud.

He's insane, Billie thought. *My uncle is insane.*

She stood from the couch, backing away into the shadows.

I shouldn't have come here.

"You're funny, princess. *Real* funny. You want answers, but all you do is blame your sorry, drunk uncle. I see how it is," he whispered, face clouding with anger. "*I see.*"

"Tell me," she said, "what exactly did she do to you? What made you want to kill her?" She took a step forward, teeth bared. "Just. Tell. Me."

She clutched the knife in her hand, fingers trailing the blade.

"You didn't know your mother," he whispered, running a hand through his long, ratty hair. "She hardly knew herself."

"That's not what I asked," Billie snapped.

He drew back at her words, turning away.

"I'm going to ask one more time. Wh—?"

"I hated her!" he screamed, pounding his fist on the coffee table. "Everyone loved *her*, everyone pitied *her*, not *me*! Not the brother wallowing in his own pity, left to drink his life away. No one cared a thing about me. Only *her*."

Billie's mouth fell agape at his words.

A motive. He's given me a motive.

"Uncle David, did you harm her?"

Silence.

"Did you *kill* her?"

No answer.

Billie watched him, his eyes bugged out in anger.

He could have killed her. My uncle killed my mother.

A laugh escaped him, long and rasping. He gasped for breath, holding his side.

Fury billowed through her. Billie clenched her fists, mouth a thin long line. Her dad had always been right about him. He deserved everything he got. He'd taken her mother away from them.

And he *laughed*.

"I can see it perfectly," Billie said, "you killed her, disposed of her body somewhere else, and then left her car at Springs Bridge, making it appear as if she committed suicide. And the fisherman—did you pay him to lie?"

"Not me," he giggled, his smile wider than ever before. "Your daddy."

10

REVELATION

BILLIE STOOD IN the middle of her dad's room, his key clutched in hand. She heard his heavy footsteps trudging up the stairs, two at a time.

Closer...closer...*now*.

"Did you pay Mr. McLain?" she asked as he stopped in front of the doorway. His face dropped, surprised to see her there, the key in her hand. *His* key.

"This if off limits. What did I tell you—?"

"Answer the question, Dad," Billie whispered. "Did you or did you not pay the fisherman?"

Her dad's face clouded. He sailed across the room,

eyes blazing. "Give that to me."

John Hagen snatched Billie's hand and pulled her closer, putting his hot breath in her face.

"*Stop!*" she screamed, writhing in his grasp. He tried to pry open her fingers, reaching for the key.

Billie swiped him across the cheek, digging her fingernails into his skin.

He fell back in a jolt of pain, a cry snagging in his throat.

Billie fumbled for her knife. She pointed the weapon at him, backing away. Her breath came out in heavy rasps, heart drumming in her ears.

He's going to kill me. Just like Mom.

Billie's dad stared in disgust. His eyes were stone cold. He rubbed where she had struck him, blood trailing down his arm.

Billie looked at her fingernails. They were wet with blood.

"Where were you on the morning of October 12th?"

"Billie…"

"Where were you, Dad?"

He shook his head, plopping down onto the bed. A sigh escaped his lips, slow and steady. When he looked at her, tears brimmed in the corners of his big, brown eyes.

"Don't do this to me."

"Did you pay the fisherman?"

Another sigh, longer than before.

"Did you kill her?"

"I'm not doing this again."

"Answer the question, Dad!"

A shake of the head. A muffled whisper.

"Was it both you *and* Uncle David?"

"No," he whispered.

"Why did Uncle David send her the threats? Or was that a lie, too?"

"He never meant it. Not any of it." He looked back up at her. "Neither did I."

"Tell me what happened," she said, lowering her weapon. She took a slow step forward. "Can you do that?"

No answer.

"Dad, please…"

Silence.

"I can't do it anymore," Billie muttered, voice cracking. "I have to know, Dad. Why can't I? Why does it have to be a secret? Why did it have to lead to this?"

It seemed like forever before he spoke. His gaze traveled throughout the room, resting on the boxes where her mother's secrets lay packed inside. A perfect bundle of the past. A perfect bundle of *her*. All he had left of the woman he once knew. If he ever knew her at all.

Perhaps this was his plan from the start, ending his daughter the same way he ended his wife. Burying the truths in another room, and locking away the evidence forever.

"Your mother never jumped from that bridge," he said, letting out the answer in one long breath. "Your uncle never meant what he said about her, and I never did anything to harm your mother, in any way."

He paused, his lips trembling. "It's all lies. Crafted from the truth; from what I've tried to keep secret for so long. None of us meant anything by it. She *told* us to do it."

"What? I don't understand…"

"Your mother. She's—"

A car pulled into the drive, the tires crunching the gravel.

Her dad's mouth closed, swallowing the truth.

She had been so close…but now she might not ever know.

"I'll get it," Billie mumbled, heading down the small, spiral staircase toward the front door.

In one long, smooth motion, she pulled the door open, and glided out across the porch, facing the figure who stood on their doorstep.

Billie's breath caught. Her heart stopped.

It was like she was staring in a mirror, an older version of herself reflected back at her. The same calm smile. The same wavy, blond hair; same chilling, blue eyes.

Her mother.

11
WISHES

BILLIE FELT SOMETHING loosening, a heavy weight lifting off her shoulders.

"Billie…"

The word drifted through the air, ringing in her ears, settling itself in her entire being. A spoken truth, by a mother who hadn't forgotten her, one who still remembered. One who came back.

"Mom?" Billie's voice trembled, a haunting whisper.

I thought you were dead.

The sentence weighed on her lips, perched on the tip of her tongue.

Billie swallowed it back.

Before she knew it, she was in her mother's arms. She wanted to hold her and never let go, keeping her there where she couldn't fade away again, with no promise of a goodbye.

Billie knew she was crying, knew she was crying harder than she had ever cried in her life. Her tears soaked her mother's shirt, pouring down Billie's cheeks, her hands, dripping into her mouth. It was a mess, but it was pain. It was beauty. It was everything she ever loved, holding her in her arms. It was five years devoid of a woman whose smile was still locked inside her head, whose voice had sang her to sleep more times than she could count.

Only now could she finally rid the image of her mother's inevitable spiral into the murky, dark waters of her death.

Billie didn't know how long they held onto each other. It felt like hours. Days.

Her mother lifted her chin, making Billie stare into those blue eyes that she knew all too well.

"Come on, I need to show you something."

She took her daughter's hand in hers, leading her away. They drifted behind the house, to the field nestled against the southern pines. Billie knew where they were headed even before they'd taken the first step.

It was a field of dandelions where her mother first showed her how beautiful the world could be. They used to always come here, talking away the hours, losing track of time. It always seemed like the world revolved around them and their words, and everyone listened.

It was only after she disappeared that Billie realized how different the place felt. It wasn't the same. Nothing was. Every time Billie returned, it only reminded her of the mother she'd lost.

The field was a broad expanse of land, dandelions as far as the eye could see. The sun shone through the trees, spilling its last few rays throughout the clearing. It wouldn't be long before the place succumbed to darkness.

Her mother sighed, letting go of Billie's hand. She stared ahead at all she left behind, her eyes glistening with tears. "Some see a weed, others see a wish."

It was what she used to always say, a constant reminder to Billie that something's true identity didn't have to hide its beauty. That there was something beautiful in everything; that there was beauty in them all.

Billie's head still spun at the shock of her mother's return. She wanted to explain every emotion, every feeling she'd ever experienced since her mother went missing. But she had a sense that the woman kneeling among the dandelions already knew; that she'd gone through it all before. They were both one and the same.

"I always dreamed of the day I could come back to you. The day I could come home. It hasn't changed," her mother said with a smile.

But that was where she was wrong. It *had* changed. And it would never be the same again.

Billie watched as her mother turned to look at her, her eyes glinting with a smile of their own. It was like the picture in Billie's bedroom had come to life. The one of her beaming as if she didn't have a care in the world;

her long, clean blond hair hanging over her shoulders.

"Where have you been, Mom? Why did you leave? I thought you were…"

She couldn't force herself to say it, to unleash that dreadful word in such a beautiful place, at such a beautiful time.

"Come on," her mother said, patting the ground beside her. "And I'll tell you."

Billie complied, waiting for Candice's words. It was like everything in the world rested on her answer.

The time was now. The waiting was over. Her mother was about to let out the truth. Billie should have felt ecstatic, relieved that she would finally get the answers to the gnawing questions she'd built her life around for the past five years. Yet why did she feel nervous? Why did she feel scared?

"I know it's been tough. Not knowing. Having to accept that I wouldn't be coming back." Her mother paused. Her lips quivered.

Billie noticed something new about her. Something that felt wrong. Her mother's accent had evolved, morphed into something foreign Billie couldn't recognize. It had lost its southern charm, replaced with a crispness that hadn't been there before.

"Five years ago, I uncovered something that put my life at risk. It was a tape. On it, a confession. To a murder."

Her mother faced her. "*My* murder."

She took in a long breath before beginning again. "This group of people had a plan to kill me. They'd thought it out, orchestrated it down to the wire. They wanted me to find the tape. They wanted me to know what they were going to do. They wanted me scared. Paranoid. In fear for my own life, knowing that at any time, they could strike. I tried to contact the police, but the killers warned me that if I did, they would get rid of anyone who had any special relation to me. Starting with you."

Billie's breath caught.

She did it to save me, Billie thought. *She left to protect me.*

"I knew that I needed to leave before they killed

everyone I held dear. I burned the tape, destroying the evidence. No one could know. Not even you.

"I told your dad, and together, we staged my disappearance. We made it look like a suicide, leaving my car and purse abandoned at Springs Bridge, hiring the fisherman to confess he'd witnessed my death. Doctors held records of my depression and suicide attempts. It all supported the theory that I'd jumped, taking with it the sorrows of my past.

"Although, things didn't go as planned. Your uncle was tasked with making it look like someone was out to get me, supporting the claim that someone pushed me from the bridge. But the police were onto him, and he had no choice but to come forward and proclaim his innocence. It was all to throw the killers off my trail, to make them think I was dead. To keep my family safe."

When her mother was finished, Billie didn't even realize she was crying. Her tears soaked the ground, dripping onto the dandelions.

The truth was painful. It hurt like a thousand swords ripping into her side. Someone wanted to kill *her*. Billie.

A seven-year old at the time. *A little girl.*

The news was almost too much to bear. She cried for her mother, for what she'd done to keep them all safe; she cried for her dad, who couldn't have stopped it from happening, who'd had to keep it from Billie against his will; and she cried for herself, knowing that she could've died before her life ever really begun, without ever knowing what she'd done to deserve it.

"Why'd you come back?" Billie asked when she was able to speak without losing it. The sentence was like a thorn, cutting her on its way out.

Candice sighed. "It's been a long time."

Billie rested with her mother's answer, hoping it would be enough.

"The thing is, I can't keep you safe. I thought I could, by taking it all with me to a different place, away from you. But it followed me back, and it'll follow you, just as it did me."

"What about Dad? Did he know you were coming back?"

"He knew everything." Candice leaned closer, her

breath blowing against Billie's ear. "He's known every move I've ever made. But I couldn't let him tell, could I?"

"These people…will they try and take you away from me again?"

"Billie." Her mother said it so peaceful. So delicate. "A bunch of people will. *The town* will. But I'm not going anywhere. I won't leave again. I could never leave you again."

Billie hoped she would keep her promise. That was always the hardest thing: making people stay.

Her only wish was that these people would leave them alone. And that they'd be safe. But she had a feeling they wouldn't. Not for a very long time.

. . . .

That night, Billie slept with her mother. Her dad had given up his spot, even though Billie wished they could all fit together, one big happy family reunited again, just like how it used to be.

The closeness reminded her of when she was little. It made her feel safe, safer than she'd felt in years.

The sweet fragrance of her mother's hair and perfume was just as Billie remembered. She nestled closer, leaning her head against her mother's chest. It was just like they used to do, before Candice drifted away, leaving only her ghost behind; one that haunted Billie's dreams; one she always saw if she looked close enough.

Billie's fingers trailed through her mother's blond hair. Candice's eyes were closed, but Billie hoped she was still awake.

"You never told me goodbye," she whispered.

Moonlight edged across the sheets, illuminating Candice's face. Her hair seemed to glow.

"Mama?"

Her mother didn't stir.

Billie's fingers grazed Candice's cheek. They trailed along her jaw and down her chin.

This isn't real, she thought.

Billie caught one last glimpse before closing her eyes. She breathed in her scent, cradling her mother's hand in hers.

There was something so peaceful in the way she fit

perfectly in her mother's arms.

12

MONSTERS

BILLIE RAN. HER lungs felt like they were going to explode, but she had to keep going, no matter the cost. Her life depended on it.

From what she was running, she didn't know. Only that if she stopped, it was over. And she would die.

Dandelions crunched beneath her feet. She was in the field, the one behind her house.

Something said her name from behind. No…someone.

She turned to look, regretting it the moment she did.

Her mother was racing after her, hands reaching for Billie in the darkness. Her hair seemed to glow, eyes shining. Even her teeth glinted in the moonlight.

Only, it wasn't her mother. It looked like her—the wavy, blonde hair, chilling, blue eyes—but the smile was all wrong, the voice unrecognizable. It was a monster, disguised as her mother. And it wanted her dead.

When Billie turned around again, she tripped, making impact with the hard ground. Her mother was on top of her in a flash, and all Billie saw was red.

....

Light spilled into the bedroom through the cracks of the blinds.

Billie's eyes fluttered open, searching for her mother. There was only an indentation of her on the cotton sheets.

Candice was gone.

Billie's heart raced. She could hear it roaring in her ears, could see it pounding in her chest through her flimsy nightdress.

Billie tried to shake the nightmare from her mind. She could still feel her mother's teeth sinking into her, the monster's nails drawing her blood.

It's only a dream, she thought. *Only a dream.*

She crept out into the hall, her feet barely making a sound. She spied the back of her mother's figure, sitting across from her father on the sofa. Their voices were drawn to a whisper.

"Who are these people?" he asked, lifting her chin to look him in the eye.

"I don't want to do this. Not right now."

The wooden floorboard creaked beneath Billie's weight. The whispers ended. Her mother turned.

"Billie," she breathed, the name itself a sigh of relief. "Come sit with me."

She nodded, rushing to join her when a heavy knock at the door stopped her dead in her tracks.

She paused, hands held out in front of her, pulse pounding in her ears.

They're here. To take her away again.

Her mother headed for the door.

"Mom, don't…"

But it was too late.

Billie surged forward, hoping she could get there in

time, at least to put up a fight, to show them who'd they messed with…

The door opened. A hand shot out.

"Candice Hagen?" a deep, resonating voice croaked.

A burly police officer stood in the doorway. He held out a hand, willing her to shake it.

She obliged.

"I'm Sheriff Dailey of Henry County. We received an anonymous tip regarding your return. We need you to come down to the station to answer some questions."

Billie's heart sank. She knew this would happen, but not so soon. Why now, when her mother had just returned to her? She couldn't let her leave. She couldn't let them take her away. Again.

Billie started to speak but Candice cut into her words. "Do you mind if we do it here? Is that alright?"

The sheriff stared at her. "I guess so."

He motioned for the others.

A young, female cop stepped through the entrance, followed by a tall, stern-looking man with a menacing scar perched above his right eyebrow.

Captain Tillman.

Billie recognized Ginger first. It was the one who helped her remain calm after the shooting in Richard Welch's home. The one who listened to every word she spoke during the interrogation. The one who bore a strange resemblance to her mother.

The captain pushed right past her, wearing his snarl like it was a part of his outfit. He stared at her mother with questioning, doubting eyes.

Billie knew him well from Mick's descriptions. She remembered he was the one who hadn't believed Mick when he informed him his sister was still alive. Billie knew the same would happen now. Accepting that this woman really was Candice Hagen would be his last resort.

A patrolman was stationed outside, for *what* Billie didn't know. Perhaps it had something to do with keeping out the others who might have already heard about her mother. News traveled fast, and if someone had spotted her slip into town, then the whole world may know by now.

Sheriff Dailey took the large recliner and the other two sat on the sofa at her father's request.

"The girl, she can't be here," Captain Tillman said with a sneer.

"Billie," her mother said. "Can you excuse us?"

She wanted to say 'no', to stand her ground and protect her mother from these cops with their shiny badges and intrusive questions, but her lips betrayed her.

"Yes, ma'am," she muttered.

She slinked away up the spiral staircase, stalling in hopes she could hear the first of their questions. They waited for her to leave.

That was okay...she would hear the whole thing. If they didn't want her there, then she wouldn't be. At least, not within sight anyway.

She sat on the top step, propping her arms on her legs. No, she wouldn't miss a thing.

Her mother cleared her throat. "I know you have a lot of questions..."

"Mrs. Hagen, we don't even know where to begin."

The silence lasted for what felt like minutes.

Finally, as if realizing she had to give them *something*, her mother let the words spill. She didn't leave anything out, even adding in a few extra details unknown to Billie. She held onto every word, wondering if the police would accept it, if Captain Tillman would even give her a chance to finish.

Fortunately, he did. But the moment she was done, he fired off the first question. Billie could almost imagine him grinding his teeth and leaning forward, acting bigger than the coward he was. She hoped to God her mother could see right through it.

"Do you realize the hundreds of man hours we've spent looking for you? And now you just show up, acting like nothing ever happened. The likes of you—"

"Enough."

The sheriff's voice seemed to rattle the house. Captain Tillman ignored his command.

"I want us to move back to the thousands and thousands of dollars we've spent on you! What crimes are you covering up, Mrs. Hagen?"

He spat her name like it left a sour taste in his

mouth.

"I told you already. It was about the tape."

"There's no proof!" he shouted. "There's nothing to indicate whether you're telling us the truth. If someone was after you, why would you come back?"

Unnerving silence settled over the living room. Billie listened for a hint of what was to come. She imagined them closing in, like a pack of rabid dogs.

The sheriff intervened. "We're looking into whether charges need to be filed on you and your family. Your husband, your brother, and Mr. McLain have lied in a criminal investigation. The State Attorney's office will determine if the statute of limitations have been met."

"We're done here," Billie's dad muttered. "Next time we meet with you, it'll be with our lawyer."

"John…"

"No, Candice." Billie could almost see him standing over them, pointing toward the door. "Get out of my house."

"Let's all calm down," Ginger said, her soft voice soothing the suffocating tension swelling in the room. "I think the first thing we forgot to do was tell Candice we're happy she's home."

Billie let out a sigh of relief she didn't know she'd been holding. If there was anyone who could bring a little more civility to the table, it was Ginger.

"The news media will make a circus out of this. It'll be our job to try and stop it."

Captain Tillman snorted. "It's not like anyone doesn't know."

The room reverted into stillness again. Billie couldn't help but wonder what they were thinking.

"We'll be meeting with the State Attorney's office tomorrow morning to see if charges should be filed," Sheriff Daily said. "We'll call in the next day or two to schedule an appointment with you. You need to make yourself available, and you need to show up. Is that clear?"

"Yes, sir," Candice said.

Billie could hear them heading for the door.

"When everyone hears of your return, we can't guarantee you how they'll act. A town can only take so much."

Her mother beat down his words. "This was my choice."

Billie gripped the rails of the stairway.

Her choice. One that left both her and her father behind. To grieve. To ponder. To haunt them in their dreams.

It was a choice Billie was still having a hard time accepting—one riddled with questions.

How did her mother know it was safe to come back? Why now? Did she know the threat had passed? That the killers had given up?

Billie had accepted her mother's answers, but the more she heard them spoken aloud, the more it made her wonder.

The mother she knew wouldn't leave her, no matter the cause. The woman she remembered wouldn't trade her for the world.

Yet why did it feel like she had?

13

WHISPERS IN THE WIND

CANDICE HAGEN WAS everywhere. She stared up at Mick from the front page of the newspaper. She flashed across the screen on the ten o'clock news. She was the topic of conversation from sunup until sundown, her name carried with the whispers in the wind.

She truly was a living, breathing "ripped from the headlines" story.

Her picture was the same one that'd been hanging up in the town for years, nailed to power lines, trees, and lying battered on the pavement, as if no one cared anymore; as if she truly was forgotten. It was an image of Candice in a field of dandelions, the one that made her seem like the happiest woman in the world. They were all the same, her smiling face marked 'missing.'

Mick used to see it all wrong, like everyone wanted him to: a beautiful, charming lady that everyone loved and admired who deserved nothing that ever came her way.

But if he looked close enough, he could see the secrets sparkling in those sinister eyes, hidden behind that too perfect smile. No one was ever like the picture made them seem.

The brisk autumn air greeted him as he stepped out onto the porch steps of their small brick house. The morning was just beginning.

Mick whisked away on his bicycle, through the streets and country of Summersville.

The town hadn't fully awakened. Restless eyes peered out at him through dimly lit bedrooms, with curtains as long as veils. The creamy sweet smell of magnolias drifted with the breeze, the only sound the peaceful low of cattle.

What a disgrace, Mick thought, that in just a few hours, Candice Hagen would ruin it all.

Mick didn't know what to think about her return; didn't know how he was supposed to feel. Was he supposed to act like the townspeople, with their feverous gossip, and false rumors? Or was he supposed to act like Clara, keeping it in where only he could know?

First his sister, and now her. How many more of the dead would return?

As the minutes passed, and the people drifted from their all-too comfortable beds to their porch swings, they were suddenly reminded of her. The air filled with her name, ruining the perfect morning. To Mick, even the scent of the magnolias seemed to turn sour, the cattle loud and insistent, all at the mention of a woman who was supposed to have died five years ago, so they could forget, so they could pretend to move on.

They were no longer silent on her tragedy. Instead, it was more alive than ever before.

"Why Summersville? Why here?"

"She's putting us through Hell…"

"Why couldn't she have died?"

Whispers. Dabbled in rage and misperception. They were all questions he was wondering himself.

Mick turned down a side street. He strolled to the last house along the end of the street, parking his bicycle in the grass. He headed for the entry.

The doorbell alerted the people within to his arrival, its shrill pitch ringing throughout the house, bouncing off the walls and ceiling.

Perhaps he'd interrupted the murmurs of *her.*

The door slipped open a crack. An eye stared out at him, before opening to reveal a short, thin woman in a lace nightgown. A smile formed on her lips.

"Mick!" the woman said, wrapping him up in her arms.

It felt so good to be home.

"Let me get the others," she squealed, sprinting away into the back of the house.

And then, there they were, rushing to meet him.

His foster family.

"Bubby!" the little blonde thing of curls squeaked

beside her mother. She latched onto his leg, burying her face in his knee.

Mick picked her up, swinging her through the air like he used to.

"Again, again," Olivia cheered. A doll with wispy locks of golden hair was clutched in her tiny hands. She held it out to him.

"For you," she said, her lips upturned in an infectious smile.

"For me?" Mick exclaimed. Olivia giggled, darting farther back into the house.

"Don't just stand there," the man to his left called. "Come in!"

"Thanks, Mr. Evans."

"Please," he laughed, running a hand through his sandy, blonde hair. "Call me David."

He ushered Mick inside, taking one last cautious glance outside before closing the door behind them.

He didn't know what had his ex-foster dad so on edge. Maybe Candice Hagen was making everyone paranoid.

A faint trace of cinnamon hung in the air. There was a candle burning in the parlor, a small flame swaying at the slightest movement.

Mick examined the walls lined with family portraits; studied the floor where the carpet met the wood. He took it all in again, confronting the memories of when he lived here, climbing up the rickety stairs that led to his room; playing board games with Olivia; pressing his ear against the wooden door to catch a snippet of one of Jessica's secret conversations with her boyfriend.

"How are you holding up?" David asked, taking a seat beside his wife on their plush, white sofa.

Mick looked away. He didn't want them to catch him staring.

"Fine. You?"

"We're doing okay," Mrs. Evans said, her classic cheesy smile plastered across her vibrant face. The pattering of feet in the hall caught Mick off guard. He turned, the outline of a child illuminated by the rising sun from the windowpane behind. Mick's breath hitched.

"Tucker?" Mrs. Evans said, her squeaky voice like a shrill whistle.

The boy stared, then ran away, slipping up the stairs. A few seconds later, Mick heard a door slam.

Mick's door.

Stop it. This isn't your home anymore.

Still, he couldn't help but feel a little pang of envy.

"Sorry, Mick. What were you telling us?"

I wasn't telling you anything.

"I don't know," he said. "I can't remember."

"How is Clara?" Mr. Evans quirked an eyebrow.

"She's doing okay. Better than expected, given that…"

Mick stopped. He swallowed.

"You don't have to talk about it, Mick. We just want to make sure—"

"They found new bullet holes. In my family's car." Mick bit his lip. "They matched the police. The FBI wants to reopen the investigation. I guess you can say we have a lot on our plate right now."

The Evans nodded, their gazes falling to their laps.

Still, he knew what they were thinking. So much had been going on his life during the time they'd opened their doors to him, and it hadn't let up. It was still happening, in some shape or form.

"It never goes away, does it?" Mrs. Evans' voice was quiet, the only other sound that of the ceiling fan overhead, slicing the air. "It's an endless ripple. We can never escape."

Mick stared. He hadn't expected her to be so vulnerable. So open. Maybe they knew more than they let on.

Her husband nodded. Something flashed in his eyes —a distant memory, maybe?

"This town is cursed," he whispered.

Suddenly, Mick didn't feel like he was welcome anymore; that he was a stranger in his old home. His gaze flicked back to the portraits; the ones with smiling faces and memories that he couldn't help but resent. They were the perfect family. The kind that adopted children and gave them a place to stay. They didn't seem to have a single fault about them.

If Mick looked deep enough, he saw it, though; the way Mr. Evans' eyes drooped like he'd lost one too many night's worth of sleep; the way his wife's smile faltered with every photo.

Of course, he knew he was wrong to believe they were perfect. One of a kind.

He still remembered Mr. Evans' words on the night they'd returned home from the police station. The confessions of his past that made Mick question everything he thought he knew about the man he trusted.

Secrets hidden behind a smile. Buried deep in the past and shrouded with a false sense of identity. Hung up on the walls for all to see, lurking just beyond everyone's vision. Hiding in plain sight.

If only he could get a closer look, at least have one more second...

If he could just get to the core of what made Summersville beat; explain the tragedies that kept happening in a town where nothing was supposed to go wrong.

Mick couldn't trust Clara, so then how could he trust them? He couldn't, especially now, when he knew that everything in this town was connected.

Candice Hagen's disappearance. Her return.

The hijacking gone wrong. His name being changed to please a criminal.

His foster family's past.

The truth would change everything.

But what was a lie? Where were the answers?

Who could he trust, when everyone had something to hide?

"Mick?"

A voice from the stairs made his thoughts dissipate. A teenage girl stared back at him, her fingers curled around the railing.

Jessica.

She nodded in his direction, heading back up the stairs. "We need to talk."

Mick's chest tightened. *Talk...him? Her?*

He cut his eyes toward the Evans, making sure it was alright. They smiled and waved him away.

He followed after her, his mind considering every possibility.

What was going on here?

When they made it to the top of the staircase, she turned to him. "I knew you would come back."

Mick's jaw dropped. "I'm not following…"

"Come on," she laughed, her fingers taking hold of his arm. She plopped on the bed, making room beside her as she brushed away a rose-gold photo album that lay half-open on her pillow. "I just had a feeling."

Mick surveyed the room. It hadn't changed.

The walls were tacked with posters of the latest boyband. Tubes of lipstick and mascara littered her dresser.

Typical teenage girl.

She laid back, a smile resting on her glossy lips. Her brown bangs fell in her eyes.

"Is it weird to say I've missed you? He's not like you, you know."

"I didn't think you'd notice."

"Why?"

"You always seemed too busy for me. Too caught up in yourself."

Instead of becoming defensive, lashing out at him with cutting words, she laughed.

"You were right. I was. But I still saw things. There was just something about you that I envied. *You* were the one with the money. *You* were the one with the love and attention from my parents. You seemed to have it all, making me feel like I had nothing. Know what I mean?"

Mick cracked a smile. "Well, I guess I have that effect on people."

"I knew you needed it. Your conditions were way worse than mine. I couldn't help but feel bad for you."

Mick couldn't believe she was telling him all this. He'd lived within her home, but she'd always felt like a stranger. One he didn't think ever noticed.

"When you left," she said, "I didn't realize how much I would miss you. But I did. And I still do."

Mick nodded. "You never realize how much you love someone until they're gone."

Jessica rolled her eyes. "Okay, Shakespeare."

She gazed up at the ceiling. Her brows were furrowed. "He'll have to go, too. Every one of them who walk through this door have to at some point. That's why I hate it here sometimes. Just waiting for the next one to come and go. They never last. They always leave. And I hardly ever want them to."

Her words were painful, even if he didn't have to live them. He thought she never paid attention, when she always did.

"Anyway," she mumbled. "Thanks for stopping in for my Ted talk."

Mick couldn't stop himself from laughing. "Anytime."

Jessica groaned, lifting herself from the sheets. "I'll be right back. Need anything?"

Mick shook his head. He reached for the photo album resting on her pillow. "No, but do you mind if I look through this?"

She rolled her eyes. "I don't care. Do what you want."

As she slipped out, Mick inspected the contents, out of curiosity he might find some old family photo of the Evans life before. Really, it was just much of the same. Baby pictures of both children, their figures and features progressing and maturing with every turn of the page. Olivia running in a cornfield, chasing a flock of ravens. Jessica, holding up her driver's license, a small smile pinching the corners of her mouth.

An old, weathered photo poked out from underneath one of April and David on their wedding day, walking down the aisle. Mick pulled it out into the light.

A young boy was centered in the middle of the photograph. He had the same calming, youthful smile that his foster dad possessed now.

This boy was David Evans.

Off to the side, another boy peeked into the camera's viewpoint. Mick probably would've recognized him had it not been for the grainy, worn quality. The only thing he could make out was the child's striped, navy shirt.

Mick's heart raced. He tried to remember what his foster dad had once told him, during the night they'd returned home from the police station.

When I was your age, I was abused by someone who I thought I could trust. He was like a brother to me.

With just a glimpse at the photo, Mick could tell that his foster dad was easily around the age Mick was now.

And this boy…the one leaning in at an angle, the one he couldn't identify because of the dated, grainy filter, could also easily be the same boy who'd abused him. The same one he'd deemed a brother.

Mick's breath caught in his throat. Here it was. His red flag. His only clue.

This could change everything.

Footsteps thundered up the stairs.

Mick didn't hesitate. He closed the photo album, jumping from the bed.

Jessica rounded the corner.

Just in time.

"Listen, I've got to go."

"Wait, why? Mick—"

"Sorry…something's come up."

Taking the stairs two at a time, Mick hurried down to the front door. He hoped she wouldn't bother to check for the photo of her father; the one that was now tucked away in his pocket.

14

MISSED CALL

THE PHONE RANG off the hook.

Billie didn't bother answering it anymore, after realizing the extent of the town's hypocrisy. The first few were from worried, curious locals who claimed her mother had been on their mind "every dreadful day that passed."

The others were those of the relentless media, who wanted to exploit Candice for a story, either to schedule appointments for interviews, or bookings on the news. Even without her consent, Candice ended up on there anyway. Whether out of curiosity, or just plain sympathy, everyone wanted to express their feelings for Billie's mother, even if they secretly wished she remained in the past, to store away in the back of their mind forever.

Almost a week after her return, the truth finally settling in Billie's mind, it still felt odd, like there was something missing. Something...out of place. It wasn't obvious, not like a taint stain on a white rug, but more like an image slowly shifting out of focus. Maybe it had something to do with her mother's story, which had too many holes to count. Or maybe it had something to do with her father, with his growing distance and few words.

Why, after his wife had finally returned, was he acting stranger than ever? It wasn't like he was just now learning the answer behind her disappearance...no, he'd held onto it the entire time. Was he struggling to accept it? Was he finally seeing her mother for who she truly was, for who she'd always been?

Whatever the reason, Billie couldn't help but notice his shift in the other direction. She'd expected him to smile more, for there to be a little extra dose of life behind his once wild and youthful eyes. Yet now, he seemed older than ever. Bags bulged from beneath his eyes, wrinkles creasing his weathered, once-handsome face. It was like the secrets were taking him down with them, a little more with each passing day.

"Dad," Billie said one morning, before her mother joined them on her usual spot on the sofa. Billie hadn't slept with her mother since the first night, which felt like a lifetime ago.

"I want to apologize. I'm sorry for never believing you, for thinking you were someone you were not. I feel ashamed, now more than ever. Please forgive me."

It was an eternity before he spoke. His face drooped, his mouth sagged. He looked sadder than ever before. Why, though? Why *now*?

"Don't apologize. Don't ever apologize." There was a coldness to his voice, fierce and cutting. "Why should you, when it's always been me?"

"But it hasn't, Dad." Billie was almost begging. Pleading. "You never left me. Not once."

His voice fell to a whisper. He looked away. "I wouldn't ever leave you. That's one thing you can count on, Billie Hagen. One thing...you can count on."

He yawned, leaning against her. It wasn't long before a soft snore escaped him.

Billie stroked his face, running her fingers through his hair. She'd always thought of her mother, of how she wished one day to hold her again.

Only now, she wished the same for her father.

She laid her head against his, thankful that both wishes had finally come true.

. . . .

"Bye, daddy," Billie whispered from the doorway. The front door shut behind her, leaving him completely alone. She didn't want to leave. She only wished to stay.

"Let's go," her mother squealed. "Have some time for ourselves." She pranced ahead, swinging her car keys along.

Billie sighed.

Shopping. They were going shopping. The word itself made Billie want to gag. She hadn't been in five years. For most of her childhood, she wasn't accustomed to the actions of a regular girl her age. Skipping through aisles of clothes, trying on the perfect outfit in hopes of catching a few eyes at school, or stressing about her waistline in dresses that lived to impress, just wasn't what she had in mind for "time to herself."

Seven years old. The last time she'd been shopping with her mother. Christmas, Easter, Halloween. The only memories she held of their time dedicated to a day at the mall. The least she could say was yes.

Cars were parked at the end of the drive. Some bore logos of TV stations; others were those of the police. Reporters snapped pictures of them as they sped past. Officers followed behind them in their unmarked vehicles.

Billie wondered how it felt to be her mother, knowing the world was caught up in her mysterious life. Did she even consider the effects her return would cause? Or was she watching it all through the rearview mirror, only speeding up when the time came?

Questions piled up inside of her, forcing their way

out.

"Where'd you go when you left? Who *were* you?"

Her mother responded faster than she'd expected, as if she'd thought of this in all the time she'd been gone, practicing her answers in the dark of a cheap motel room.

"I drifted in and out of different places. I preferred the West. It was new. Different than here. I had a job as a bookkeeper in Tucson. Worked as a waitress in a diner in California. But I was always afraid someone would recognize me. Finally, I realized that five years was enough."

"So you came back?"

"Yes."

"What was your name?"

Her mother exhaled, leaning back in her seat. "I had many. One for every place I traveled. A new accent for every place in between."

"How about dad? Will they file charges? Will he be taken away?"

"Possibly," she said, like it didn't matter. "It'll take

them a while to decide. A few weeks at best."

Billie nodded, even though it wasn't what she wanted to hear. "I found some things while you were gone. Records of suicide attempts, prescriptions for depression and anxiety. Mom, why were you unhappy? Why did you want to—?"

Billie swallowed, forcing the word out. "Die?"

Much to her surprise, her mother smiled, taking Billie's hand in hers. She looked her in the eye, flashing that smile of hers, one that didn't even seem real anymore. "I didn't realize what I had."

Even then, her mother made something so ordinary sound like a mystery.

. . . .

The closest shopping mall was in White Springs, the next town over from Summersville. They crossed Springs Bridge, with its shallow waters and secrets sweltering underneath the rising sun.

Billie thought about asking her mother why she'd chosen such a location for her staged suicide, but she knew now wasn't the time. She'd asked enough.

The reporters exited their vehicles as Candice pulled to a stop near the entrance.

Microphones were shoved in Billie's face as she slammed the car door behind her, questions coming from every direction.

"How does it feel now that your mother has returned?"

"Did she give you the answers behind her disappearance?"

"Is she the same as you remembered?"

"Get out of my way," Billie spat, deflecting them off of her like a swarm of pesky insects.

"Ready?" Candice beamed, taking her by the hand. It felt forced, as if it were only for the cameras capturing their every move.

Billie could almost see the headline, with her mother's hand wrapped snugly in hers—one that read: Reunited At Last.

If only they knew how much she was trying to tug away.

Billie didn't understand why her mother thought this was a good idea. Why would she want to go somewhere like this, knowing people would berate her with questions? Why did her mother seem so happy after knowing what she'd all put them through? Why was she so willing to chance going out in public?

But when Billie looked at her mother, she understood. Candice's lips were parted in a shy smile, eyes bright and burning with a fire, almost like she was guilty of something, like she knew exactly what she was doing. Billie shouldn't have questioned it—of course her mother enjoyed the attention. After five years of hiding away, hoping no one would recognize her, now she could be the center of it all, she could be *known*.

A reporter pushed past the crowd, rushing up behind them.

"Candice, would you like to be a part of a special episode regarding your homecoming? All questions will be solely decided by you."

Billie knew who the woman was even before she got a glimpse of her plastic face, long, blond braid, and cold, reptile-like eyes. She snatched the business card from the woman's hands, ripping it in her face. She threw the remains at the reporter's feet, flashing a sneering smile.

"We don't deal with snakes."

Billie sashayed away, her mother's hand held proudly in her own. It was only as they entered that Billie knew they'd made a mistake.

"Candice?" a woman whispered, her mouth dropping before their very eyes. A minute before, she'd had her hands pressed against the glass, staring out at them as they arrived.

"It's you...you're back...Candice...it's me... Stephanie...your friend...your old co-worker..."

The woman was spastic, wrapping her mother up in a long embrace, tears falling on Candice's pale face.

"Stephanie...yes, I remember...we were nurses...you —"

"I just can't believe it," she cut in. "It's you. It's really *you*. You haven't changed...you look exactly the same. How have you been? *Where* have you been? Oh my, I just *can't* believe it..."

"Mom?" Billie said, grabbing her arm. "I think I

found a dress. I want you to come see."

She hoped the lie would be enough to distract the pressing stranger. But it only grew worse.

"Can I get a picture...please, Candice...you would do that, wouldn't you?"

"I need to go. I'll see you arou—"

"Candice?"

Another woman spotted them, her eyes widening. "Look, Josh," she whispered, nudging the man beside her, "It's the missing woman! You know, the one I've been telling you about."

Not a second later, a crowd of people surrounded her mother, trapping her within their tight circle. Their voices rose above her own, toying with their victim.

Billie watched in shock, slowly backing away. She couldn't save her mother. Not this time. Not now.

A man pushed her out of the way, rushing to the front of the horde. Billie stumbled onto the floor. Tears formed in her eyes.

No one noticed. No one checked to make sure she was okay. All eyes were locked on her mother, her name intensifying like a droning beat, pulsing with the voices of the crowd.

A name the town would be hearing forever.

15

LIGHTS OUT

8:30.

Mr. McLain's heart quickened. Blood pounded in his ears. His appointment began in less than ten minutes. He couldn't be late.

The doors to the small bus opened as he hurried down the steps, even though hurrying was an overstatement. His cane held him up...no, *the pain* held him up. His legs were leaden, his feet stomping along as if oversized military boots were attached to them. It required much effort to speak, but even more to force himself to move.

"See you in an hour," the somber voice called from the passenger seat.

Mr. McLain grunted in response. If only he had the energy, the willingness...

You can't give up, the nurses at his residential home told him. *It'll only get worse.*

They didn't understand. Not until they were his age. Giving up felt like the only alternative.

He stumbled along, relying on the cane for balance, his breaths coming in heavy rasps.

Everything was an effort. Nothing felt possible anymore. Yet he continued on, as he always did, like his nurses wanted him to, whisking him away on the small shuttle bus that always seemed to lead him to bad news.

Alzheimer's. A growth in his stomach. His near-crippled state. Everything his doctor was monitoring.

Sometimes, he could remember, more than he used to. His recall had sharpened, his memory more alert. But it seemed every time he went back, they found something else wrong. Who knew what today's news would be.

The waiting room to the small doctor's office was empty. A clock on the wall read thirty-five minutes past the hour.

I have time, Mr. McLain thought. *But I'll have to be quick.*

Moving as fast as his legs would allow him, he exited through the door and down the long hallway leading to the restroom.

The last tendrils of light dissipated as the door slammed shut behind him. Darkness cloaked the hallway, thick and heavy. It surrounded him from every side, pressing on his senses.

He ambled down the corridor, grasping for the wall. His eyes were trained on the glowing, red exit sign at the other end, the only source of light.

The only sounds were those of his cane prodding against the floor, though he thought he heard footsteps heading toward him in the inky darkness. He hastened, his breaths rattling within his throat. It seemed to last forever until his hands grasped the cool, metal knob. He stumbled inside, the light almost knocking him back. It was blinding compared to the pitch-black.

Mr. McLain headed for the stalls that lined the left wall, joining the dirty sinks with their cracked mirrors.

The lights flickered, then descended into darkness. Mr. McLain cursed, standing still in the middle of the bathroom. His fingers swiped for the light switch, but paused when there came a sound from the door.

Footsteps. The lock clicking into place.

Someone was there with him. Waiting in the dark.

"Who—who's there?"

A cough. Right behind him.

A hand clamped over his mouth, pulling him farther into the shadows.

No...not a hand...*cloth*...a handkerchief...

The grip tightened around his face. Cloth filled his mouth, his nose, muffling his cries.

Mr. McLain's eyes fluttered. His breathing slowed.

The last thing he heard was his head crack against the hardwood floor.

. . . .

Today was not the day for death.

Not for Mr. McLain, and certainly not for Ginger. She wasn't ready for it, *wouldn't* have been ready for it if that had been the case. Summersville couldn't handle anymore. How much more of it all before it led them to the breaking point?

Ginger pushed back the curtains of the hospital bed, preparing herself for what she was about to see. The fisherman was still breathing, even after the medics found him, passed out on the floor of the bathroom, his head bloody and bruised from the fall. He'd been in a coma ever since.

He lay sprawled out on the sheets, his hair hanging over his face, making the contusion on his head all the more noticeable. His head was swollen, a purple bruise spread across the left side of his face. A needle in his arm was connected to an IV bag, which dripped a steady dose of fluid into his veins.

He was barely hanging on.

"Ginger?"

The young cop turned, noticing a frail man in a bulky white coat, sweeping the tops of his shoes. His hair was ruffled, a blemish of red on his cheeks. Ginger knew it was just one of those days.

"I can't prove that he has any injuries sustained by another person. It appears as if he fainted, evidenced by the contusion on his head."

"You don't think it was inflicted by someone else?"

The doctor's eyebrows rose. "Are you insinuating an attempted murder?"

Ginger sighed, slumping against the wall. Why couldn't anyone keep their nose in their own business?

"That's what I'm looking into."

She studied the limp form in the bed. Mr. McLain was unresponsive, caught in a place where she couldn't reach him. She wondered what he could tell her, if only he were awake. "Mr. McLain?" she whispered.

"It's no use, ma'am. He can't hear you."

Ginger ignored the doctor, inching closer.

"You think it's strange…that everything has to happen when *she* comes back?"

She had to admit, it *was* strange. Yet even stranger was the crumpled piece of paper clutched in Mr.

McLain's balled fist.

"It's crazy, what they're all saying about her. She's not the same…"

Ginger heard the doctor's words, but was focused primarily on the paper poking out between Mr. McLain's fingers. She didn't have time for Candice Hagen, not now anyway. Everyone was wrong about her, including the man standing a few feet away. She was still the same woman she'd always been, even with the rumors circulating like a weathered, dusty fan gathering speed. They'd never known her. They were just too blind to notice.

Just because a woman returns, doesn't mean she has to be any different. And just because a woman disappears, doesn't mean she has to be dead.

"What are you doing?" the doctor asked, watching as Ginger pried the man's hand open.

She smoothed out the wadded paper, spying the two words scrawled on the dirty note. The doctor peered over her shoulder.

"What does it say?" he whispered.

Ginger didn't answer. She continued to stare at the clue grasped in her shaking hands.

Kill me.

16

SMOKE

THE CREAK ON the steps was not supposed to wake her. Not even that of the door opening downstairs, a faint breeze bristling through the silence of the midnight hours.

Billie watched from her bedroom window as her mother slinked to the burn barrel on the edge of the towering wood, a glow emanating from her fingertips. The match plummeted into the depths of the rusty metal, setting it ablaze.

Papers were consumed by the flames. Old I.D.'s. Driver's licenses. Her mother's every name and past life all carried away in a plume of smoke. Drifting into the night, the evidence succumbing to ash.

....

The Summer Café buzzed with activity on the afternoon Mick and Billie decided to meet. Customers shuffled in and out, plastic cups clutched in their greasy hands.

The restaurant had been around for decades, spanning back all the way to the 1920s. It was truly the only place around for an affordable, home-cooked meal.

Checkered barstools lined the main counter and oak tables sat beneath a dim, overhanging lightbulb. None of the tables accommodated more than four people, however, the waitresses liked to combine them for the large group of old men who congregated there for the daily lunch special.

The two kids made their way to a spot in the corner, away from the others. The space was almost devoid of light, except for the distant glow of the burning bulbs. It was the same place John and Candice Hagen had sat years prior, whispering their conspiracies to one another in the darkness. The spot was perfect for the discussion of crimes. Thirsty for decade old-secrets. Famous for lies.

A pretty, young blond waitress practically skipped to their table. She looked barely older than them.

"Heeeyyy, what can I get y'all to drink?"

"I'll take some sweet—"

"We're fine, thank you," Billie chimed in. There was an edge to her voice.

The waitress looked deflated, her face drooping before their eyes.

"Dingy as a church bell," Billie muttered under her breath as the girl hurried away.

The waitress darted back and forth throughout the place, large cups of the café's famous vanilla shakes tucked between her elbows, along with steaming hot bowls of the daily soup balanced on her arms.

Her eyes flicked back to Mick and Billie, as if they might respond to the delectable treats. The kids paid her no mind.

"I could've gone for some sweet tea," Mick mumbled.

A couple of tables away, a man shuffled through a newspaper—the Henry County Examiner. On the front page, the headline read: *Attempted Murder in Summersville.*

"Billie, do you know anything about—?"

"The fisherman? Yeah, everyone's talking about it."

"Even after Candice Hagen—"

"Mick. Don't you get it? My mother returns. A man is almost killed in a public facility. Connect the dots. It has everything to do with her."

"The tape," Mick said, recalling Candice's story from the news. "Someone was after her."

"Someone is *still* after her. It isn't a coincidence that the prime suspect in her disappearance is almost dead when she finally decides to come back."

"But why him? He doesn't know about the tapes, does he?"

"He knew why she left, remember? My dad paid him to keep her secret. Maybe there's something else we're missing. Something my mother doesn't want anyone else to know. Maybe he got caught up in it and the people behind the tape found out."

"A secret to kill for?"

"Possibly." Billie's voice grew quiet. "She told me she couldn't keep me safe anymore. First, it was the fisherman. Who knows who it will be next."

Mick's eyebrows rose. "They're targeting everyone involved in her disappearance, aren't they? But why? Isn't it all said and done? The tape is gone. The fisherman is practically dead."

"She's still here. That, in itself, is bigger than anything."

"So you're saying they're not going to stop until she's...*dead?*"

"Exactly."

"Even if that means getting rid of anyone who could possibly know about the secret she uncovered on that tape."

"That's the thing." Billie leaned forward. "On the tape, she discovered a reason for her death. They were threatening to kill her. But why would they do that in the first place? Just what did she find that made them want to keep her silent?"

Mick sighed. "It's a mystery."

"No. It's my life."

Her expression hardened, the corners of her mouth pinching together. The shadows spilled across her face. Her eyes glowed in the dark.

"I used to think when I found out who did it, who killed Mom…"

A low moan escaped her. Her words were strangled. Weak.

Mick turned away.

"We don't have to talk about this."

"…I thought I could finally be at peace. But now that she's back, she's… different. What if we've gotten this all wrong?" The shadows seemed to have crept in closer, hanging onto her every word. "What if I never knew my mother at all?"

Mick reached across the table and grasped her hand in his. It was the closest they'd been in weeks, ever since the world had moved on without them. He knew that if he let her go, she might slip away forever.

"You were seven when she left," he whispered. "Then, you only saw what you wanted to. You never looked beyond the surface. Now, you see her for who she truly is, for how she's always been. It's her, Billie. Believe me."

She pulled away. "I don't know what to believe anymore."

Billie let out a sigh, eyes squeezed shut. "You know, after she left, nothing was the same. I wasn't. My dad wasn't. It's like when my mom left, I had to learn how to live again. I'd gotten so attached to her that I didn't know what to do. My dad didn't talk anymore. The house felt smaller, distant. Everywhere I looked, she was there.

"One time," she said, her voice breaking, "I thought about ending it in the field behind our house. But I stopped myself. For one reason only."

Mick didn't even breathe. "Why…why didn't you?"

A tear leaked down her face, spilling into her open mouth. "Because of you."

Mick swallowed. His hands trembled at his sides. "I

don't understand."

"God, Mick." She smiled. "You were the only thing I had. And if I would've left, I knew you wouldn't understand. I knew what that would have done to you."

"We were just kids."

"We still are."

Mick couldn't stop the smile that spread across his face. "Thanks, cowgirl," he laughed. "For staying. I don't know what I would have done if you had left."

She winked. "Anytime."

"I'm always here, you know. If you need me."

"So am I."

Silence settled between them, the only noise that of the swinging kitchen door as their waitress hurried in and out.

Mick's fingers grasped the photo stored away in his jean pocket, the frayed edges rubbing against them. He dropped it down in front of her.

"I found something that I think might prove interesting."

"Another mystery?" she asked, inspecting the photo.

"I remembered something my foster dad told me. That's him as a child. On the right is someone who might have abused him when he was in foster care. Can't be too sure, though."

"Who is it?"

"No clue. The image is worn. It's hard to tell."

"And you think this might be who, exactly?"

"I don't know." He smiled. "But I'm going to find out."

She handed the photo back, her words mirroring his thoughts. "This town's covered up so much."

Mick shook his head. "But we won't let it. Not anymore."

17

CREAK ON THE STAIRS

Rain pelted the window.

Billie stared out into the night, watching the lightning flicker above the trees. Her mother sat close by. Upstairs, her dad was sound asleep.

The wind blew in gusts. The rain fell faster, like tiny bullets, pounding the glass.

Something scraped against the window.

Billie's throat thickened with fear. Her breathing slowed as the realization hit her.

A tree branch. Limbs like claws, reaching for her.

"Scared of a little storm?"

Her mother stared at Billie over the top of her reading glasses. A book rested in her lap.

Billie bit her lip. She wasn't scared…she was uptight. And it wasn't because of what was taking place outside. "I want to know more. About the tape."

Candice sighed, setting her glasses on the coffee table as she leaned back in the recliner. "I know you're scared. I know you want answers—"

"It's not that. It's what you're not telling me."

The corners of her mother's mouth twitched. "And what's that?"

"Why would someone want to kill you?"

She shook her head. "Rage, jealousy, greed. There's many reasons why one would take the life of another."

"That's not what I asked," Billie snapped. "Was it because of me?"

"Billie, please. Not everything's about you."

"Right. Because it's only ever been about *you*."

Her mother's fists clenched. She tried to force a smile, but it made her look like she was writhing in pain.

"I saw you last night."

Surprise flickered in her mother's eyes like a flame. "You don't know *what* you saw."

The lights shimmered. Thunder resounded outside, a crack of lightning filling the room. The wind howled.

Candice never broke Billie's stare. "Why do you act like this? You used to never *be* like this."

Billie's eyes narrowed. "I could say the same for you."

The house groaned as it descended into darkness. The tree limb slammed against the window more ferociously now, as if to claw its way in.

The recliner squeaked. Billie watched her mother slink through the darkness to the mantle. A beam of light spilled from the flashlight gripped in her hands.

There was a creak on the stairs.

Candice whirled around. "John?"

The creaking stopped. Only silence remained.

"Dad?" Billie called, her feet barely making a sound as she crept to the spiral staircase. She turned to Candice, her voice a whisper. "Turn the light off."

They stood in the dark, flashes of lightning

obscuring the pitch-black. Billie thought she heard another creak, just above her.

"Something's not right," Candice said, her hot breath blowing against Billie's ear.

Through the roar of the storm, Billie heard the sound of a person's ragged breathing, followed by a cough echoing in the darkness.

"Someone's here," Billie said, her hands gripping the railing. "Someone's in the house."

Fingers grasped her skin, cold as ice. "Take my hand," Candice whispered.

Billie obeyed, backing across the floor, trying not to make a sound. Her heart was like a bomb, ticking away in her chest. At any moment, it would burst.

Footsteps pattered down the stairs.

Billie froze. Her hand fell from her mother's grasp.

The footsteps came closer, the breathing more ragged now.

Billie knew one thing: it wasn't her dad.

Her mother pulled her back into a storage closet. The door was left open a crack. Billie peered out as a figure stepped down from the stairs.

A scream ripped from Billie's throat before she could stop it. Candice's hand pressed tight against her mouth.

The figure turned. In the flashes from the storm, she could make out something in the intruder's hands, lightning glinting off the metal.

A long, jagged knife.

Billie didn't dare move. She didn't even know if she breathed. She was sure the intruder saw them just down the hall, closing in for the kill.

He was so close now that Billie could smell his breath, could hear the whistling of his raspy breaths.

A hand reached out for the closet. The knob turned...

Something crashed upstairs.

"Candice?" a familiar voice called, footsteps racing down the stairs again.

The knob clicked back into place. The figure darted down the hall.

John Hagen rounded the corner. Candice pushed past Billie, hurrying to him. "John?"

She fell into his arms. "I thought you were—"

Glass shattered from the back of the house. Her dad rushed ahead. Billie followed the flashlight beam after him.

He was standing in the middle of the den, his eyes trained ahead.

"Dad?" Billie let go a shaky breath. Glass crunched underneath her shoes.

They stared out into the night, the back door banging wildly in the wind.

18
QUESTIONS

"YOU HAVE NO idea who this could've been?"

Ginger scribbled away on her notepad. Candice stood in the middle of the cops, her head in her hands.

"An ex, a co-worker, or…"

Captain Tillman stopped, his mouth a thin long line. "Your return has left a lot of people confused. Angry, even. Someone might be trying to threaten you. Is there anyone in particular you think might have…?"

"No," Candice said, taking a seat on the porch swing. Billie watched from a distance, straining to hear their words. Her dad was being questioned by another detective in the house. "It's them. It's the people I told you about. They want me gone. They want me dead."

Candice's tears glistened in the moonlight. She gazed off into the yard, a wild look in her eyes. The rain was now a faint trickle. It dripped onto the pulsing red and blue lights in a corner of the lawn.

Candice groaned, running a hand through her messy hair. "I should have never come back here."

Captain Tillman glowered down at her. "This is what I'm having trouble with. If these people were really after you, they would have already gotten you by now. Tell me if I'm wrong," he said, his voice rising with every word, "but I think there's something you're not telling me."

Billie glided across the porch, her hands balled into fists. "Listen up, Scarface," she spat. "Someone broke into our house. Someone could've killed us, yet all you care about is your own pointless fantasies."

Candice sighed. "Billie—"

"Don't tell him anything, Mom. He doesn't deserve any bit of news that comes his way."

The cop laughed. "Like I'm taking advice from some puny, little girl."

Billie swung her arm through the air, but a firm hand reached out and pulled it behind her back. "Drop it," Ginger barked in her ear.

Billie swung away, her hands shaking out of anger. How badly she wanted to add another scar to that ugly face of his.

"Come with me," Ginger said, pulling Billie away to the other side of the porch. "You need to stop. I would hate if I have to take you away in handcuffs."

Ginger gestured for Billie to sit, but she only continued to fume.

"I don't want him here. He's just going to take her away again. Dad, too. I'll be just like Mick...with some foster family. But what does he care? What do any of you care?"

"He cares, Billie. He just has a funny way of showing it. Look," she said, "we're not picking on your parents in any way. They made choices. We can't help that. You can't help that. They haven't been telling the whole truth. If they had, we wouldn't be here right now. We're just doing our job."

"I just don't want you to take them away," Billie said, falling into Ginger's arms. Her tears soaked her uniform, but the cop didn't seem to care. "They're all I have. I can't be alone."

"And you won't be. Everything's going to be fine. Trust me."

Billie nodded. "Okay," she breathed, wiping the tears from her eyes. "Okay."

"Billie? What's wrong?" Candice rushed over, staring down at Ginger like it was a crime that a cop could be hugging her daughter in such a way.

"What are you doing?" her mother hissed. "Get away from her. Now."

"Candice—"

"You heard me. *Go.*"

She pulled Billie behind her. Billie tried to tug away, but her mother wouldn't let go. She only gripped harder.

"Leave my daughter out of this," Candice sneered as Ginger walked away. "This doesn't have anything to do with her."

Ginger turned around again, shaking her head. Billie could have sworn she'd heard her whisper the words, "But it does."

19

CONFESSIONS

THE NIGHT WAS silent. The storm was now a dull throb on the horizon, shimmers of lightning blinking in the distance. The cop car droned down a dirt path. The air was calm. Still.

The perfect night for murder, Ginger thought.

Cornstalks brushed the hood of the vehicle. Lights dimming, Ginger watched as the car swerved off the edge of the road. It crawled to a halt.

"Tell me what you know," Captain Tillman said, powering off the engine. The car hummed, then faded away into silence.

"About what?"

"Mr. McLain."

Ginger faced the window, staring off into the depths of the cornfield. She thought she saw a shadow move in the distance. Perhaps it was just her tired mind succumbing to a dream.

"There were no cameras. No witnesses. Only a note. And the victim, well…he isn't talking."

"Do you believe her?"

"Who? Candice? No."

"What are we missing then?"

Ginger held onto the question, willing herself to untangle every thread, every lie, into something they could understand. She came up short.

"I don't know."

"Sure?"

"I think both crimes are connected. Mr. McLain. Candice. Someone tried to kill them. Why, though, I don't have the answer to."

"*Why?* I'll tell you why. People like that think they can get away with anything. Like nothing will ever bother them once they've committed the acts they've built inside their head for years, wallowing in it until they hold the gun in their hands and pull the trigger. No, they don't even begin to know how to carry out a crime."

"And you do?"

Captain Tillman turned to look at her. His eyes blazed with a confession. "You, of anyone, know the answer to that."

"I'm sorry, I—"

"Don't you remember?" His lips parted into a twisted grin. "Why would you let yourself forget?"

"Don't say it. *Don't*."

The captain laughed. A dry, throaty laugh. Accusing, mocking her.

Her breaths were shallow. Sweat trickled down her brow. "Why would you say that? Why would you *ever* say that?"

Ginger couldn't stop the images that flooded her mind. The gunshot. A night under the stars ending in violence. Bloodshed. *Murder.*

"I know what happened," Captain Tillman whispered.

"He didn't mean to, *he didn't mean it*—"

"He should've gone to jail."

"Stop. *Stop* it."

The car started again. Ginger stared at the headlights like it would burn away the rage searing through her.

Captain Tillman edged closer, his face inches from her own. "You should know better than anyone."

20

FLOWER IN THE THORNS

THE FISHERMAN WAS awake. He sat fully alert, hands gripping the sheets pulled around him, eyes glimmering like they held answers.

Ginger drew in a breath, reading the two words scrawled into the slip of paper for the hundredth time. *Kill me.*

He must have awakened for a short time, long enough to write the note, before drifting back into his coma.

The doctor informed her of Mr. McLain's full recovery as soon as he could. The news had felt like a lead itself, even before Ginger had shown up to the hospital to receive the answers from her victim, who, days prior had almost died in a pool of his own blood, taking his secrets with him, and letting a murderer slip away to strike again.

The once purple bruise on the side of Mr. McLain's face had faded to yellow. His long hair had been neatly combed back, unlike the last visit, and the swelling from his wound had diminished to the size of a bottle cap. Ginger promised she'd keep the questions simple. He was still unable to talk.

"Mr. McLain, did someone attack you?"

His head trembled on his shoulders. *Yes.*

"Did you write this?" Ginger held up the note.

He nodded.

"Someone tried to…to kill you?" she asked, referring to her only clue.

Again, another nod.

Ginger cleared her throat, giving him a warm, calming smile. "Can you tell me who did this?"

In response, he took a pen off the station beside him

and began to write.

....

The bag crinkled in Clara's hands as she took her prescription from the cashier. The woman stared a second too long. When she finally spoke, there was a tremor in her voice.

"H—have a nice day!" Instead of cheerful, it came out flat.

Clara noticed the eyes following her as she left, the humid afternoon air thick and muggy. The heat sweltered on the strip of businesses along downtown Summersville. Clara couldn't help but remember a month ago, when she'd ventured here after catching a ride from the woods.

She recalled the wail of the siren. The pulsing lights of the cop car. The homeless man.

It all seemed like it happened years ago. Time seemed to move by slower now that she was free. Maybe it was because she'd gotten so accustomed to the hours spent in her cell. Back then, the days faded into another, followed by hours of daydreams and sleep.

Now that she was living in reality, she was struggling to keep up. How was she supposed to stay up to date when she'd missed over a decade of the world? Was there a chance she could move on, pretending like the last eleven years never happened?

All that time away made her feel like an outsider. A drifter. A stranger. She'd felt like she'd crawled in a dead girl's skin, seeing everything for the first time. She didn't have the memories most women her age cherished for a lifetime, when they were young and the world seemed to revolve around them. What she'd been left with was what most would call a nightmare. The memories of her childhood were becoming harder to conjure. They were shifting images, fraying with each day since she'd escaped. Her mind wouldn't be able to hold onto them much longer.

Tea parties with her sister. Hunting and fishing with her dad. Shopping sprees with her mother on a plot of land that had evolved into something unrecognizable. Her family and their memories had been erased in the time Clara was gone. Now, the only proof of them lurked in the deadest of places: in the house left to rot and decay in the middle of town; in the headlines stored away in a growing stack at the library, hiding in plain sight.

Summersville had moved on.

"Clara?"

A man stared up at her from the street. His clothes were ragged and filthy, his face speckled with dirt and grime. His cracked lips upturned in a smile, revealing the few teeth he had.

The homeless man.

Her arms were wrapped around him in a flash, pulling him close. A familiar sensation prickled on her skin. She forgot the way it felt to be remembered for who she was.

His grip tightened around her, his breath hot and foul. "She's back," he whispered.

Clara let him go. She looked at him as if she had never seen him before.

"What I told you about her—"

"—is safe. I'll never tell."

Vehicles ambled by, pedestrians stopping to gawk as Clara sat beside him. Maybe he was different in their eyes. Maybe they saw a man who deserved the life that he had gotten, left to scourge for food and a place to rest. But it didn't matter, none of it mattered. To Clara, they might as well have been just two old friends, finally meeting up again to pick up where they'd left off.

"Ya don't have to do this…"

"Please," she smirked. "None of them mean anything to me."

He chuckled, ignoring the people snapping pictures of him as he did. It was like they were in on a secret that no one else knew, gathering the proof of a legend, that a man like him could be happy, even with the life he had received.

"How have you been? Haven't been causing any trouble have you?"

The man shook his head. "Naw, not lately. I should be askin' ya the same thing."

She sighed, leaning against the brick building. It felt like years were between them. "Everything's changed. It's not the same."

"It never'll be. Even now that she's back. They're still all pretendin'," he said, pointing to the tattered "Missing" poster caught on one last piece of tape in the storefront window.

The woman's eyes made Clara shiver. She hoped to have gone forever without seeing that face again.

"Who were you?" Clara asked. "Before you ended up here?"

In all their time spent together while on the run, she had never even learned his name. Maybe he had built up enough trust to finally tell her, resting with his answers until they met again. Or, maybe he knew the truth would turn her away.

"Promise me somethin'," he said.

"What's that?"

"That you won't judge me. Not like the others. I'm not proud of anythin' about myself. I'm bruised worse than the lot of ya."

"I'll understand," Clara whispered. And in some twisted way, she would. It couldn't be any more damaging than her own past, one where she could never escape the man who wanted nothing more than to kill her. Mr. Welch used to watch her in the darkness, always when he thought she was sleeping—she could always tell by the raspy breathing—even though she couldn't see him in the dark.

"I used to be a cop," he mumbled. He grew stiff, his hands clenched at his sides. "It was in another town, not too far from here. Not too different by any means." He paused. There seemed to be a fire burning behind his eyes, the past taking him with it and swallowing him whole. "I knew what they covered up. Knew what they hid. They decided to let me go after I learned somethin' that I shouldn't've. There's always a price to pay when you're that far up in the law."

Something edged in Clara's memory. The bullets ripping into her mother. Her neck falling limp.

The police had done it. No one ever knew.

"There are secrets in every town," Clara whispered. "Even here."

"No. Here, they're everywhere."

A tear slid down his dirty cheek, splattering on the pavement. "I killed a man. In front of my daughter. We used to sleep outside some nights, with the sounds all around us. We felt safe...calm. Like the woods would protect us."

He shook his head. A tear fell onto Clara's lap. "He'd been watchin' us for weeks."

"Who?"

His words came out like a thorn, jagged and sharp. "The sheriff."

Clara drew in a breath. She laid a hand on his shoulder. "You don't have to do this—"

"He wanted me to pay for what I'd learned. For the secret I'd uncovered. For what I threatened to expose."

"Please...*stop*—"

"He almost killed her, ya know. He almost got my daughter. It's the only reason I didn't get locked 'way somewhere.

"After all of it 'appened, my wife left me. She took our daughter with her. Ever since, I've been tryin' to find her. I want to tell her I'm sorry."

Clara didn't know what it was—maybe the guilt she felt over leaving this man, the utter devastation he had to endure, or the way his tragic past resembled her own —but she wanted nothing more than to help him find his daughter. She took his hand in hers.

"She left to become a cop for 'erself. She wanted to protect people, wanted to be like her daddy. 'Course, I didn't try an' stop her. Even though she was taken from me, a parent has ta let their child go at some point or 'nother. You have to let 'em see the world for them self. She'll see one day, if she hasn't 'ready. Every town has their secrets. And the people who try ta enforce the law can be just as bad as the ones who break it."

"You could have gotten a job, you could have turned your life around. You didn't have to end up on the streets."

He seemed to ignore her for a while, watching the cars pass by and the children playing in the street. "My wife gave up on me. So did my daughter. It was 'nough to make me give up on myself."

"But you can change it," Clara cried. "You can

become something better…"

"Why?" he snapped. "Why, when the people you've looked up to your 'tire life turn out to be like the ones rottin' in their cells? And why, Clara, when the people ya' love leave ya' to beg for everythin' ya' once had? I'm done with it all. I've lived it."

Clara was almost pleading. "Listen to me—"

He cut her off, brushing her away. "So when someone like ya' self comes 'long, ya' hate to let 'em go. Those who make ya' feel a little more human. A little more loved."

Clara stopped, her eyes filling with tears. "I didn't realize I was like that."

He smiled. "Ya' didn't give up on me. Ya' told me your secrets. That was more than I could ever ask."

They sat there for a long while, resting with the other's answer. They watched the life bustling in their small town, and they couldn't help but wonder why their lives weren't spared like the others, why they'd had to watch innocents die while others lived free; why they had to live in cells and in dungeons, while others got to drive away, taking their loved ones with them.

Maybe they were both prone to damage, or maybe they were chosen because no one else could survive it like they could.

Either way, they were slowly repairing, piece by piece; a flower sprouting from the thorns.

"What's your daughter's name?" Clara asked, like his answer could hold the meaning to everything.

"Her name," he said, his eyes glinting as his mouth parted into a smile, "is Ginger."

21
INTRUSION

THE HOUSE WAS no longer fading. It didn't seem to halfway exist like it used to. In the days of Clara's return, she did all she could to salvage her memory of the place.

She'd painted one room her mother's favorite color —a speckled, rusty green that somehow reminded her of the sea. For hours, she'd brushed and decorated until her fingers ached, until memory seemed to spew out of her like a rolling wave. When Clara was finished, and the wall shone a speckled green, she realized she'd painted something else. Two figures were molded into the wall, a child's hand in that of her mother's, shimmering with the waves.

It was her sister, Abigale, with their mother. The image replaced those of their shattered forms, their life seeping onto the autumn leaves. It reminded Clara that they were okay; that they were together, with nothing to harm them now that they were in their favorite place.

The next day, Clara had reverted to cleaning. She'd gotten on her hands and knees, and with a bucket of soapy water and an old dish rag, she scrubbed the baseboards, ridding them of dust and mildew. In the kitchen, she used ammonia, stripping the twenty-year-old wax off the tile floor. With years and years of pent up energy, the work was stimulating. The house no longer smelled vacant and forgotten.

She still had weeks' worth left to do, rooms to be washed and reconstructed. The wallpaper peeled in her old bedroom, the moth-eaten drapes flimsy and torn, and the blinds tilted and tired, hanging on by a single thread. The walls had outgrown its skin, falling into itself, the air stale and musky, riddled with dust. It would be awhile before Clara could repair it like she wanted.

Over the course of several weeks, she'd transformed the inside to where it was almost livable again.

She knew she had to let her family go, let them fade back into the walls, leaving them to rest. She tried harder every day.

Clara opened the paper bag from the pharmacy. She unscrewed the lid off her prescription, downing a sleeping pill.

"You're dealing with the aftermath," her doctor told her after she described her long, restless nights. The hours where she had trouble falling asleep and staying asleep.

"You're suffering from insomnia," her doctor said. "It's understandable. Most of my patients who've endured a life-altering event experience it as well."

His words stung. Clara didn't like someone telling her what was wrong; she'd gone through enough of that on her own. She knew she couldn't help it. Right when her head hit the pillow, all the horrors came springing back.

She could no longer sleep in the dark. There were too many things there that she couldn't see, watching her like Mr. Welch did when he thought she was asleep.

Sleep. It was worse. Sleep led to nightmares, where those who had died were now living, and the places from her past had returned. When Clara closed her eyes, confronted by the darkness, she saw shifting shapes and images swirling through the black. Those who had died, and those who had killed. Faces of the innocents and captives. Her past was more alive in the dark.

"When will it go away?"

Her doctor said he didn't know. He said it might not ever.

And then there was the question that made her numb: "Why does it hurt worse now that I'm free?"

He'd tried to explain. He'd tried to make her understand. But his reasons weren't enough.

Clara pulled the sheets over her as she crawled into bed. There was a tugging behind her eyes, a weightlessness to her every move. The pills were beginning to work.

A floorboard creaked in the back of the house.

Clara closed her eyes. A minute passed in silence.

Just before she drifted away into restlessness, there was a drawn out squeal from the kitchen.

Just the boards expanding, Clara thought.

Her eyes closed again.

Another creak. Just outside the door.

Clara sat up, every move an effort. She didn't have any energy now that she'd taken the drug.

Her heart pounded in her chest. She swallowed.

It's just the pills. Playing tricks.

That's when she heard it: footsteps. Slowly trekking through the house.

Clara tried to make as little noise as possible. The bedsprings groaned, giving her away.

She searched through the drawers of her night stand, finally spotting something she could use. She held the object up in the light.

A long, handheld mirror.

Clara grasped the cool metal of the doorknob. She almost dreaded to see what was on the other side.

It reminded her of her escape from the cell. Pattering up the stairs. Grasping the knob. Her ear pressed against the door, straining to hear any indication of someone waiting in the next room.

She licked her dry lips. Every beat of her pulsing heart throbbed in her ears. It was all she could hear.

Slowly, she stepped out into the hall.

Something was wrong.

A flicker of movement captured Clara's attention. She stifled a scream, throwing the mirror before she could even think.

It shattered as it made contact with the wall. Glass shards scattered across the floor, cutting through her skin as she tried to run away. A hand clamped around her throat.

Her fists swung aimlessly through the air. The grip around her neck only tightened.

"Let. Me. Go," Clara sputtered.

Cold eyes peered down at her. Thirsty for revenge.

She sunk her nails into the intruder's skin. He howled, slapping her across the face, the sound like the crack of a gunshot. She fell out of his grip, lunging for the knife she kept in the kitchen drawer.

Her fingers tightened around the blade. She stabbed upward, a slice through the air, missing him by inches.

Clara didn't hesitate. She slipped across the tile floor and slammed her bedroom door, but a hand caught it from the other side, forcing it open. She gritted her teeth, her hands planted against the door, pushing with all the strength she had left. Finally, the door clicked shut.

Her false sense of security was short-lived. Wood splintered as the door exploded inward, and Clara covered her head with arms, dodging the wooden pieces as the door came off its hinges.

Adrenaline kicking in, she stabbed the blade toward her assailant, but another hard slap across the face deflected the blow. Nails ripped through her cheek, tearing flesh.

A scream stuck in her throat, as if one of the intruder's large, strong hands had a firm grip around her vocal cords, squeezing them until she choked.

In one flinching move, he wrapped his hands around Clara's neck and shoved her body backwards into the dresser mirror. Shards ripped through her shirt as the glass crunched and shattered, scraping the sides of her face and sinking into her skin. She hit the floor with a thud, glass stabbing her from beneath.

Her body ached, matching the throb of her heartbeat, a searing pain coursing through her with every breath. She felt like she was on fire.

"Please," she rasped.

Her fingers stretched for the knife, but he kicked it away across the glass.

The drug had slowed her down. She lay bloodied and broken beneath him, waiting for the blow that would finally end her.

Clara watched as he snatched the blade up, plunging it down to where she lay, cutting off her screams.

. . . .

The sky waned. The night tugged the light away, pulling back the curtain to reveal the stars.

Mick was on one of his afternoon strolls. He let his

thoughts drift away with the dusk, clearing his mind and thinking of nothing in particular. All that time of staying cooped up in their cramped little house was stifling, especially with the past hiding in every crack of the crumbling walls.

He strayed to the countryside, where the trees opened and the fields rolled with the hills. The air wasn't as heavy here. The atmosphere wasn't as crippling.

Here, he could finally breathe.

The air smelled of cut hay and honeysuckle. Cows grazed in the pastures, sheep roamed in the valley, crickets buzzed from the sawgrass in the swamps.

Every now and then, there was the haunting call of an owl, or the growl of a beast unknown to his ears.

Mick saw the police car before he heard it, bustling down the road toward him. It came to a stop on the shoulder of the road.

At first, Mick thought it was Ginger, but when the car door flew open, he realized he was wrong.

"Mick."

The cop's face was ashen. He had the build of a

football player. His dark complexion made him blend in with the night.

Mick remembered him as Investigator Jones, the same man who'd helped him stay calm during his interview following Robert Smith's death. From some distant memory, Mick recalled that his nickname was Gator.

"I need you to come with me. *Now.*"

Mick didn't move. "What's wrong?"

"It's your sister. It's Clara…"

Mick took a step back. "I…I don't understand—"

"I need you to get in the car."

Mick's jaw clenched. "No."

"Mick!" Gator was almost pleading. He moved forward, kneeling down to Mick's height.

"Look, I know you're scared. I know it might not make sense…"

"I'm not getting in that car until you tell me what's wrong."

The cop sighed, running a hand through his untamed hair. He looked away. "Your sister was stabbed."

The world seemed to turn upside down. Mick breathed in the cold, night air, his lungs constricting.

"Is she…is she dead?"

"No. But she will be, if the responders don't hurry." Gator held out his hand. "Come on, Mick."

Clara's warning flashed across his mind. *You can't trust the police.*

His sister was right. They'd killed his mom, and they'd covered it up.

He stared into the man's pleading eyes.

He's barely older than me, Mick thought.

"Take me to her."

"I can't…"

"You will, if you want me to get in that car."

The cop exhaled. In the cold air, his breath looked like smoke.

"Okay," he muttered. "Okay."

Mick grasped the door handle, a thousand thoughts springing into his mind as he climbed into the police car.

One called out louder than all the others.

Your sister is dead.

And this time, Mick didn't fight it. He knew she was gone.

They were too late.

22

SECRETS

"Billie?"

A gentle voice woke her from her slumber. Her eyes opened.

It was her mother.

For a split second, she thought she was still dreaming. Her mother was missing...she'd left years ago...the town presumed her dead...

But when she looked into her mother's eyes, all became clear.

"Come on. I want to show you something."

Billie rose from the cotton sheets. She caught a

glimpse out the window, where the moon wavered behind a flimsy cloud.

"I need to sleep…"

Her mother smiled. "Not now, Billie."

They walked out into the night, leaving the house farther and farther behind. Billie hadn't even gotten a chance to tell her father goodbye.

The field of dandelions gleamed under the moonlight. Tiny traces of their seeds drifted in the brisk wind.

Her mother sat among them, closing her eyes and breathing deeply.

"Why are we here?"

Her mother laughed, a hint of mockery in her voice. Her words chilled Billie to the bone when she turned her head and whispered, "To get away."

Billie stood back from the woman in front of her. Since they'd arrived, it was as if the whole place had changed. Where the moon had been filling the clearing with its pale, translucent glow, it now hid behind the trees, the field falling into shadow; the dandelions now sagged, devoid of seeds. They looked wilted and tired.

Tonight, the wishes were dead.

"You can't just come back, Candice," Billie whispered.

"Don't call me that," her mother snapped. "I'm your *mom*."

Billie shook her head, the words untangling themselves and spewing from her mouth. "That woman died a long time ago."

Her mother laughed, shrill and wild. It carried with the wind, swirling through the clearing. "You've always had an imagination, *my dandelion*."

Billie's insides twisted. Her mother used to always call her that, whispering it in her ear before she turned the light out. Now, it sounded vile and foreign, like something that had the potential to be deadly.

Billie blinked. It was if everything about her mother had changed. Her once elegant blond hair now seemed shriveled and old, her once striking blue eyes now drooped, a hundred different mysteries flickering behind them.

Maybe her mother had changed, fading into this woman that Billie could no longer recognize. Or maybe she'd never known her mother at all.

"You can't live in the past, Candice. Things change. People change. *I've* changed."

Billie stepped forward. "Stop pretending. Stop looking for things that aren't there."

Candice blinked. When she looked back at her again, Billie thought she saw a little part of her mother there, just beyond the surface. "I'm sorry."

"You know how much pain you caused? How many nights Dad and I cried ourselves to sleep? How many times I searched for you, just out of hope that you were still alive?"

A tear trickled down Candice's face. "Billie."

"And now you just come back, pretending that the last five years never happened."

"No...*no*..."

"A mother doesn't just leave her daughter. No matter if there is a tape explaining why." Billie clenched her fists, her face tightening and twisting like she was writing in pain. "You didn't even leave *a note*. A note, Candice! No, you left *a ghost,* one to haunt me and toy with me, one that everyone tried their best not to see. One that is no longer what it used to be."

"They were after me. I had to keep you safe."

"Stop, mom." Billie's voice shook. "Please."

Candice sighed, and for a moment, she was her mother again. The one that loved her, and held her, and would never leave her. But when she spoke, the woman slipped away. "Tell a lie enough and people will start to believe it."

"Why'd you come back?" Billie whispered, putting her hand on Candice's shoulder. Just like before, it was as if everything in the world rested on her answer. "What's the real reason?"

"I did it for you."

"I want the truth."

Tears threatened to spill from Candice's eyes, but she blinked them away. "It was never about the tapes. Your dad always believed they were real, that I burned them to destroy the evidence. There wasn't a killer out to get me or a tape that gave me an excuse to run away. It was all staged, all lies."

Billie felt her heart breaking piece by piece, shattering more with her mother's every word. "Why would you leave me, Mom? Why? Didn't you love me?"

Candice sighed. "I loved you more than life itself."

"Then why, Mom? Can't you just tell me? Why is it so hard?"

"Because!" Her mother was screaming. "Because *someone* took it all away! My happiness, my life, my love. I didn't even want to live."

"Who, Mom?"

Candice was crying. She broke a little more with each sob, falling away onto the grass.

Then, like a switch, she sat up, her anger pushing through her pain, the name like poison on her tongue. "Richard Welch."

Billie backed away. "I...I don't understand."

"There's a lot you don't know, Billie."

"Were you working with him? Were you...were you...?"

Another thought came to mind. She didn't want to think it. She couldn't even bear to hear herself say it.

"Were you having an affair?"

Candice sucked in a breath. "No."

"What about him, then?"

"You wouldn't understand."

Billie stopped. She was done playing games. "You tell me now, or I'm calling Ginger."

"And why would you do that?"

Billie didn't hesitate. "Because you scare me."

Candice didn't laugh this time. She didn't even move. Her gaze was lost in the growing darkness, her hair flailing in the wind.

Shadows flickered at the edge of the clearing. A scream tore through the silence.

Billie's heart slid into her throat.

It's only an animal, she told herself. *There's nothing to be afraid of.*

But she knew there was.

When her mother opened her mouth to speak, it scared Billie more than anything. Even more than the creatures she knew were watching them from the woods.

"We used to come here all the time. Me and her."
Candice's voice cracked. "But now she's gone."

"Who?"

Candice turned. Secrets glistened behind her eyes.
"Your sister."

23

WAITING

THE MINUTES BLED into hours. Mick lost track of time. The waiting room was vacant, except for Gator, who leaned back in his chair, cap pulled down low over his eyes. Mick waited, his foot tapping anxiously against the floor. He bit his lip, grief swelling within him.

He'd almost seen his sister die before. He'd even embraced it, at least for a moment. But he wasn't ready. Not again. Not this time. There were too many things he hadn't said, too many things they'd never gotten a chance to do together.

He hadn't even told her goodbye.

She couldn't go…she *couldn't.*

"Gator?" Mick asked, his voice cracking. "Tell me she's going to be okay."

The cop opened his eyes. "Of course, Mick. Don't worry about it."

"I just can't let her go. You don't understand, but…" Mick looked away. "She's the only family I have left."

Gator put a hand on his knee. "No, kid. We're your family, too."

. . . .

Clara was lying on her back in a narrow bed with white linens when Mick finally got the chance to see her.

It'd been a day, one full of waiting; one where all the comfort Mick had in knowing his sister was okay were the dedicated looks on the doctor's faces as they shuffled in and out. It was the only thing keeping him sane.

Clara's face was paler than usual, a similar shade to the white sheets she laid on. Her face seemed to sag when she smiled. Even her eyes were dark and obscure.

The skin on her face and arms were cut, long, deep

gashes trailing down them. Stitches lined the wounds, like tiny thorns embedded in her skin.

Still, it replaced the image of her body splayed at his feet, right after the bullet had entered her from behind. It was better than the thoughts of her being stabbed, her cries defenseless against the jagged blade.

"Clara?" Mick asked, like it wasn't really her, just a girl who resembled his sister, so close to death.

"It's okay. I'm okay."

Gator stood in the doorway, his eyes patrolling the hall as if her attacker might show at any given moment.

Mick looked back at him, as if he might break the silence or crack a joke to ease the tension between them.

Mick took a step forward.

"How did this happen?" he whispered.

Clara's lips tightened. Her voice sounded tired and weak. "I should've told you before. You have to understand."

"What is it?"

"You wanted to know what I knew about Candice Hagen. You've wanted to ever since I came back, haven't you?"

Mick's breath hitched. He slowly nodded. "But we don't have to talk about it."

"No," she snapped. "Listen to me. That woman… she's dangerous."

"Did she do this?"

"No."

"Then who, Clara?" His voice broke. "I thought this was all over. I thought we were safe."

She closed her eyes, leaning her head back against her pillow. "That's the thing: we'll never be safe."

Water dripped into the IV bag hooked into her veins. The machine beeped beside her. Her heartbeat was spiking.

"What I'm about to tell you, I've only ever told one person before." She looked toward the door, which was now closed. Still, her voice fell to a whisper. "People have tried to kill me for my secrets, but this one is the most vital. Do you understand?"

He wasn't sure if he did. She'd told someone else before? He couldn't help but wonder who.

"You have to make me a promise." She stared deep into his eyes, taking his hand. "The police—they're not your friends. You can't tell them this. It's not safe."

"But Ginger, Gator—they're different."

"No, Mick. They can't be trusted. Our lives are on the line here."

"Are they involved?"

She didn't answer him. In some way, it was worse than if she'd told him yes.

"Trust no one. Can you do that?" Her grip tightened. "For me?"

Mick didn't know what was going to happen; what his sister was about to admit. He was anxious, scared even.

"Okay," he breathed. "I promise."

She leaned forward, wincing through the stabbing pain.

"And one more thing."

"Yes?"

"You can't tell Billie. No matter what."

"Why? She's safe, Clara. She's the only one I can

trust."

"No. She's just like her mother. I can *feel* it."

"Clara." Mick's voice cracked. "You're scaring me."

"I'm sorry," she said. "But you need to know the truth in case something happens to me. It's for your own good."

She pulled away. He could see the risk gleaming in her eyes, the truth rising into vision, one she'd tried to keep buried for so long.

Her words rang in his ears.

"Can you keep a secret?"

24
TRUTHS AND LIES

"HER NAME WAS Ellie."

Candice's tears glinted in the moonlight. "When I lost her, it felt like I'd lost a part of myself."

Billie forgot to breathe. She couldn't stop her mother's words, even though she wished they were all lies.

Hadn't she wanted the truth? Hadn't she based her whole world on it?

Now, she wished she'd never asked at all.

"Why didn't you tell me?"

"She died before her fourth birthday," Candice said,

as if that made all the difference in the world. "After she passed, I didn't want another child. I didn't want to face it again. But then you were born."

"*Stop…*"

"I couldn't lose another child. Not one like Ellie. I couldn't allow myself to become attached again. It only led to pain. I guess that's why leaving you was so much easier."

Billie shook her head. "How could you even say that?"

"But your father," she said, "he was better than me. He never once compared you to Ellie."

Candice sighed. "But me? I couldn't forget. I see her everywhere. Sometimes, I even think she's still here."

"But she's not," Billie snapped. "Stop pretending. You still have *me*."

"She was buried here, you know. In this field."

Billie wished she was human enough to care. Now she only wished her mother would take everything back.

Her mother didn't love her. Her mother loved Ellie.

"I'm still your daughter," Billie whispered. "I'm still

here."

Her mother nodded. "I know, Billie."

"Don't say my name!" The words spilled from her mouth before she could stop them. "A mother loves. A mother remembers. She doesn't *forget*. You shouldn't have ever had a child. Ell—*I* deserved better."

"It's not like how it sounds…"

"You've never loved me. You don't even care. Am I right? Say it, Mom. If you're half the mother you're supposed to be, then say it!"

"One day, you'll realize that leaving was the best thing that ever happened to me."

"I don't care anymore, *Candice*," she whispered. "Maybe the town was right. Maybe you should've died. Maybe you shouldn't have ever existed at all."

Billie leaned closer. She could feel Candice's breath on her face. "I found the prescriptions. I found your journal. You didn't care a thing about any of us. You only wanted the easy way out, just like the coward you are."

Candice didn't even blink.

"You left because the past was too real. The evidence of your suicide attempts and depression gave you an excuse to stage your death, and so you did. You decided that when you finally returned home, you would spin an elaborate story that everyone would believe. You could come back and live a happy life, pretending that nothing had ever changed. And the truth? Well, you would bury it just like you'd buried Ellie. No one would have to know."

Candice's sadness melted off her like wax. Her face was emotionless, as if Billie's words hadn't managed to reach her. Maybe she was already too far gone.

Billie wanted nothing more than to walk away. To leave. To not look back. To believe that she was loved, and that she'd always been mistaken; that her mother had died years ago in the murky waters off Springs Bridge. It was easier to believe a lie. Maybe if she left, she could bury the truth where she couldn't ever find it again.

Billie waited for something to happen. Minutes passed by in silence. One. Two. Five.

Candice's lips parted. All the mysteries from her past came tumbling out in her words, twisting and turning into one.

"I disappeared because I had to. Ellie was only a part of it. You've seemed to have already forgotten what I told you before. Richard Welch had everything to do with why I vanished."

Richard Welch.

Billie's head spun. *The fund. The shooting. The cell.*

The cell.

"It's because of Clara," Billie muttered. "It's always been about her."

Candice looked away. Her voice trembled. "Yes."

Clara—that day on her doorstep. The stranger with the baggy clothes and pale skin.

I know something about your mother.

She'd known. She'd always known.

"You were her nurse," Billie breathed. "When she got sick, you helped keep her alive. You knew she was in that cell."

"Yes."

That's what Clara wanted me to know, Billie thought. *That's what she'd kept from me all this time.*

"Mr. Welch needed someone like you to nurse her back to health. Besides, he knew he could trust you. He knew how to make you keep your word."

"It's over now," she said, like none of it mattered anymore. "That was a long time ago."

"Why'd you do it, Mom? You could've told someone —you could've put an end to a murderer. Clara could've been saved."

Candice shook her head. "He was going to kill you if I told. I couldn't risk it. I couldn't take that chance. Even if it meant setting a captive free."

"I thought you only loved Ellie."

"That's where you're wrong," she said. "A mother will do anything to keep her child safe. Even if it means going away for a little while."

"Why'd you come back?"

"Because he's dead," she whispered. "Because I finally feel safe."

Candice looked back at her. Vulnerable. Broken. "I

could've gone to jail."

"That's why you lied, didn't you? You told my dad the same story you've been telling yourself for years. Made it look better for yourself. The suicide attempts and death threats supported your story. It made it look like you took your own life, just to throw Mr. Welch off your trail."

Candice sighed. "I couldn't tell anyone the real reason. John—he wasn't strong enough to handle it. He would've turned me in before I'd even gotten a chance to leave. Besides, Mr. Welch had already made claims. He feared I would be a weak link. That I would break under the pressure. Turn both of us in. That's why I had to leave. If I hadn't, you wouldn't be here. I wouldn't even have a family."

"So you changed your name and your accent, and you left it all behind."

She closed her eyes. "Yes."

"So if the threat has passed, then why is a man lying in a coma? Why did someone try to kill us in our house that night?"

"I don't know."

"I think you do."

Candice swallowed. "Blaming your own mother…"

"Why'd you bring me here?" Billie backed away. "Where's dad?"

"Wouldn't you like to leave?" Candice stared off into the night, her gaze hardening. "With it all behind you, never once looking back?"

Fear gripped Billie's insides. She struggled to breathe, her heart roaring in her ears. "What have you done?"

Candice stood. Fire burned in her eyes. "You're coming with me."

Billie took another step back on the grass, her body trembling. "No."

Her mother held out her hand. "We can start a new life together. Just the two of us. We can leave this place behind forever. We never even have to look back."

Her face twisted, eyes burning brighter, searing with rage. "Come on, Billie," she barked. "What's stopping you? *Mick?* He doesn't care about you. He's just a damaged boy who's been using you this entire time. And your dad? He'll just find another woman to love, another daughter to replace you."

Billie's head spun. She balled her fists. "Stop it! That's enough."

"Can't you see? I'm the only one who really cares. I *came back* for you. I *left* for you. Why can't you do the same for me?"

Billie kept backing away, her mother coming closer and closer. Her hand lowered, balling into a fist.

Then they were running.

Dandelions crunched beneath Billie's feet, the trees racing by. Her lungs felt like they were going to explode, but she had to keep going.

Someone said her name from behind.

It's not her, Billie thought, her legs picking up speed. *Don't look back. Don't. Look.*

She could feel her mother's hand reaching for her in the darkness, teeth reared back to sink into her.

Any moment, she would trip. It would be over. All she would see was red.

The house lights blinked through the trees. Sticks

splintered beneath her feet. Dirt flew as she churned the soil.

Adrenaline pumped through every vein in her body. She couldn't stop. If she did, her mother would kill her.

Her own mother.

Gravel crunched beneath her. Their driveway…she'd made it to their driveway…

Her lungs burned, legs numb. She gritted her teeth, pushing through the pain.

Don't stop. Don't look back.

She darted up the porch steps. Her fingers grasped the cold metal, swinging it shut faster than she could blink.

The lock slid into place. Her mother pounded on the glass. Screaming. Pleading.

She'd almost had her.

"Billie! *Please.* It's me. It's *your mother.*"

Billie backed away from the door. She breathed, her heart whirring in her ears, lungs throbbing in her chest.

"Billie?"

The floorboards creaked. She spun around. "Dad?"

His eyes were wide. They were locked on the doorknob.

"Don't let her in," Billie said. She grasped his hand, pulling him away from the door. "I need you to call Ginger. We have to do it *now*."

"What's going on…?"

"There isn't time, Dad!"

He blinked, his brown eyes filling with tears. "I don't understand."

"You can't let her in. You have to listen to me."

Billie tried to hold him back, but stopped when something moved in the corner.

Her hands fell. She stood paralyzed in fear, the terror pinning her to the spot.

Someone was here. She could feel it.

Slowly, a figure stepped out from the shadows, a long, jagged blade gleaming in his hands.

"The whole family," Uncle David said, a crazy smile tugging on his cracked lips. "Who's it going to be first?"

25

CONNECTING THE DOTS

GLASS SHATTERED FROM the doorway. Candice pulled herself through the gap, hands bloodied and bruised.

Uncle David didn't even hesitate. He lunged forward, sinking the knife into John's chest.

Time seemed to freeze. Billie watched as her dad's mouth formed a wide O of surprise. For a brief second, his gaze met Billie's. A deep gurgle reverberated in John's throat as Uncle David jerked the knife out, his eyes rolling in the back of his head as his body fell away onto the hard floor.

Drops of blood fell off the tip of the blade. Her dad's body was still.

Billie stared in horror. A scream rose, stopping at the brink of her throat. She sputtered, eyes locked on the blood spurting from her dad's wound.

Candice looked down at her husband's body; at the blood pooling on the wooden floorboards.

She didn't even scream.

"This wasn't part of the plan," Uncle David gritted. "You were supposed to keep her in that field."

"Did you handle Clara?" Her voice wavered.

"She's good as dead."

Candice nodded. She put a hand on Billie's shoulder. "We have to go now, dear."

Billie's fist collided with her mother's face. The blow sent her reeling, slipping on the blood. She stared at Billie with hatred gleaming in her cold eyes.

"Don't tell me what to do."

Uncle David grabbed her, pinning her arms to her sides. "Let me go!" she said.

The cool metal pressed against her throat. "Don't

make me do it," he whispered.

"Dad! *Dad.*" Tears fell down her face. "You killed my dad!"

"Let her go," Candice said. A purple bruise was already visible on her pale skin.

"Is this what you wanted?" Billie cried. "Do you even care?"

"Leave, David." Candice's tone was deadly. "Don't come back."

He snorted. "Are you serious? You think I can just let you go? What are we going to do about *her*?"

"I said leave."

Uncle David sneered. "What about the body?"

Billie willed herself a peek at her dad. The blood was everywhere now, sinking in between the cracks, seeping into the old wood. He lay motionless.

Billie blinked. *No.*

She thought it was her tired mind, maybe even a trick of the light.

But she knew what she saw.

For an instant, she'd seen her dad's chest rise and fall.

He wasn't dead. Not yet.

"You were in the house that night," Billie whispered. "You were there to kill him."

The blade pressed harder against her skin. "Shut up."

"You tried to kill Mr. McLain. Tried to kill Clara."

She's good as dead, Uncle David said.

But what if he was wrong?

"You couldn't do it that night. You got confused. Thought my dad was the one in the storage closet."

"Shut. Up!"

Connect the dots, Billie thought.

"So you wait for tonight. Candice takes me out to the field. But the plan failed. Again."

"He's dead. That's all that matters."

"Billie?" Candice took a shaky step forward. "You need to stop. You don't know what you're saying."

Connect the dots.

"The threat passed when Mr. Welch died. You came back."

"Billie."

"But you forgot the most important thing. You

forgot about Clara. The only other one who knew."

"It's over. It's done."

"You need someone to help you get away with it. Besides, you're too perfect to kill anyone."

"Enough."

"So you get your brother. You know he'll do it. He'd do anything for you, just like he helped you disappear."

"He *offered.*"

"With Clara gone, you can finally live. Your secret is safe. But wait…there's others who might find out. The fisherman, for one. You knew that he didn't really know the real reason why you disappeared, but it's better to be safe than sorry, right?"

Candice gnashed her teeth. "It was just a precaution."

"Right," Billie said. "That's all it was."

Candice glared at her. If looks could kill, it'd be over.

"Your husband is another. You can't have him around. And what, were you going to get rid of me? It wouldn't matter because you only ever loved Ellie."

"That's not true."

"You know it is."

"Did you think I wanted this?" Candice grunted. "That I wanted my husband to die?"

"No," Billie said coolly. "Of course not. But people change, don't they, Candice? Living without him for five years made it easier to let him go, so you did."

Don't look at him, Billie thought. *You have to remain calm. You can't let it show.*

"What he did to me...what Mr. Welch put me through, it changed me. Made me different. I could never go back."

"That's where you're wrong. You could've told someone. You could've stopped him. You could've saved Clara."

"Okay. So what if I had? He goes to jail. Clara is free. But what about the others? Those who would kill me for giving him away? You see, he had ties with people. I knew because he told me. Mick. The fund. He couldn't let me go because I already knew too much."

She paused, her voice breaking. "He was going to kill me. The others would have, too. The librarian, the lawyer, that teacher. Robert Smith. But they're gone now. It's all over. I can finally live."

"No, Candice," Billie said. "You're going to jail. For conspiracy. For planning a murder. You're going to live in a cell for the rest of your life. You're going to finally pay."

Candice winced like she was in pain. She fell onto the stairs, head in her hands. Ugly sobs ripped through her. "I'm sorry. *I deserve it.* Every bit of it."

Uncle David spoke. Had it not been for the knife held to her throat, Billie would have forgotten he was there. "Not so fast, princess. You two aren't going anywhere."

He pushed her ahead, his knife aimed in the crease between her shoulder blade.

"Go," he barked. "Both of you."

Candice hesitated. She stared down at the body on the floor. "I can't leave him."

"He's dead," Uncle David said. Suddenly, he yanked her mother's hair back, the blade pressed against her chest. She cried out, stumbling on the wood.

He pushed her past Billie, putting his foul breath in Billie's face.

"You won't get away with this," she said, hands clenched. "You couldn't even kill the fisherman."

"Maybe not," he grinned. "But this time, I know *exactly* what I'm doing."

Billie spat, straight in his face, a thick wad of spit landing on his cheek. She tried to put up a fight as he grabbed her face forcefully between his fingers, doing anything she possibly could: swiping her nails across his cheek, kicking him in the groin.

He lifted her from the ground, carrying her out into the night.

"Dad," Billie screamed. "DAD!"

Uncle David's hand pressed tight against her mouth, his dirty nails piercing her skin.

Before the door had a chance to close, she caught one last glimpse of her dad's body.

Still, she couldn't deny what she saw.

His eyes were open.

26

SPRINGS BRIDGE

THE STAINED CLOTH seats in Uncle David's rustic Ford truck reeked of cigarette smoke. Dirty chip bags and beer bottles littered the space. Billie couldn't tell where it ended and where it began.

The truck sputtered and bucked. Uncle David slammed his fist down on the dash.

Billie took a deep breath, shoving her fear back long enough to form a question. "Where are we going?"

Her uncle ignored her, fumbling around for the beer bottle in the passenger seat. The car swerved as he drained the last of the drink.

"Why is it always gone?" he hissed, throwing it down at his feet.

Candice put an arm around her in the backseat. Billie should've tugged away. She shouldn't have given in.

But something about it comforted her. Something about the gesture reminded her of the way Candice used to be.

"We're going to be okay," her mother said.

Billie didn't know why she found herself believing it.

She thought of Mick. If Clara was dead, and if Uncle David killed her, then what about her brother? Did Mick get in the way? Had her uncle...

Billie squeezed her eyes shut so hard they burned. All she could see was red...the blood that had covered the floors...the blood seeping out of her dad's stab wound.

Panic clawed its way up her throat, like something trapped inside her wanted out.

They were going to die. Her own uncle was going to kill them. No mercy. No remorse.

Billie swallowed.

Maybe it would be different. Maybe he had bigger things in store. *Much bigger.*

A knife was too messy. A gun had too much finality.

Maybe he wanted to *enjoy* it.

It wasn't until the trees opened and the water shone crisp and dark below them, that she got her answer. The last time she'd been here, the water was barely a trickle. Now, staring down at the black waves in the center of the stream, it seemed deeper and menacing, like it was capable of hiding their drowned bodies beneath the rising flood.

Drowning was different. Exciting.

Except, what if they could swim? What then?

"Listen to me," Candice said, her voice a gentle whisper in Billie's ear. "You have to remain calm. You can't let him see what you're thinking. He feeds off it. It only makes him stronger."

Billie bit down on her lip.

Shut up, she wanted to say. *You're the one who got us in this mess in the first place. Because of you, I might not ever get to tell my friend goodbye.*

The truck crept to a halt on Springs Bridge. Billie held her breath as Uncle David powered off the engine, turning to look back at them.

He licked his lips, eyes gleaming with hunger. Revenge.

"Please," Billie whispered. "You can't do this."

So much for not showing fear.

Uncle David laughed, spit trickling down the corners of his mouth. "You're wrong, princess. This is the only way."

He lifted the lid to the console. The moonlight glinted off the metal of the gun.

"Get out."

Run.

Billie didn't know whether she should believe the nagging voice. If she ran, she wouldn't get very far. She would surely die.

But if she stayed, what good would that do?

Don't look back.

She almost did it, racing off into the inky darkness, using the moonlight as her path. But the butt of the gun hit her across the face, sending her sprawling on the bridge.

Pain shot through her hands. Tiny pieces of gravel were embedded within her skin.

"Get up," he gritted. "GET UP!"

Billie obliged, raising her hands.

It was over now. This was it.

She would die in these waters, body lost to the current. They might not ever find her.

"Please."

Uncle David moved closer, his finger placed firmly on the trigger.

Billie backed away, nearing the edge.

"You don't even care?" Billie asked. "Your own niece?"

Her uncle sneered. "You mean nothing to me."

He hit her in the chest with the gun, watching as she moved closer and closer to her death.

"Why are you doing this?" she whimpered. "Why have you *changed*?"

He glowered at her, his smile fading. "I've never

changed, princess. I've always been this way."

"Don't you remember?" she muttered, slowly inching forward.

One step. Two.

"When I was little, I used to sit in your lap and you would tell me the funniest stories. You even took me to the rodeo one time, David. That's why I fell in love with horses."

He paused, lips trembling. The gun lowered slightly.

"Yes. I remember," her uncle said, eyes sparkling with a distant memory.

"Then why have you changed?"

He snapped out of his daze, raising his gun level with her head. "Look where it all got me," he seethed. "I don't have anything you do. I don't even have a family."

"No," she said, face scrunched up like she was in pain, "We're your family."

"No, kid." He looked away, biting his lower lip. "Things have to change for me. Things need to be better. *I have to be remembered.*"

"Uncle Da—"

"Don't say it!"

His eyes brimmed with tears, his stare unfocused.

Billie stopped. She couldn't do it, she couldn't reason with a killer. Not someone who was bent on destroying her.

"Let her go." Candice stepped forward from out of the shadows. "That's my *daughter*."

Uncle David reached forward, squeezing his sister's face in his fingers, his dirty nails sinking into Candice's skin. "Don't tell me what to do."

Billie's eyes fell to the gun. She surged forward, knocking her uncle off balance, reaching for the weapon dangling in the air.

He grabbed it in one move, striking it across Billie's face. A gush of blood spurted from her nose. She fell in a heap on the bridge, pain exploding from the blow to her face.

A long strand of saliva flew from Candice's mouth. Uncle David staggered back, a string of curses escaping him.

He raised the gun, mouth pulled into a deranged

smile. "Go to hell, Candice."

The gunshot blast was inches from Billie's ear as she lunged forward, hands placed firmly in the small of her uncle's back, pushing him over the edge. His arm latched onto hers at the last second, and suddenly, she was falling.

They seemed to hang in mid-air, careening down to the water below them, her uncle's scream fading with the gunfire. They plunged into the stream, the frigid water clawing at their skin. Billie thrashed in her uncle's grasp, rising and sinking with the dark waves. Water invaded her nose, the burning liquid infiltrating her mouth.

Her uncle's cold eyes stared up at her, his grip tightened around her ankle, pulling her down with him. She kicked outward, her foot making contact with his face.

Slipping out of his grip, Billie surged through the water. Her head broke the surface as she gasped for breath.

Through the darkness, Billie noticed a form standing

at the water's edge. Before she knew it, her mother was pulling her to safety, her hand wrapped snug in Candice's clasp.

They raced to the sandbar, their legs battering the surface of the water. Her mother was like a ghost in the night, skin gleaming under the light of the moon. Her blond hair was bunched around her shoulders, flailing in her pursuit.

A body surged out of the water. Hands pulled Candice down, her cries subdued as she slipped beneath the current.

"MAMA!"

The water rippled beside Billie. She watched frantically as a body resurfaced, a cold hand gripping Billie's leg. Uncle David's teeth were like glass shards, smiling up at her.

He pulled Billie down and the waves swallowed her. The darkness pressed in, cold and black.

Billie kicked her limbs, lungs burning. Her body thrashed and spiraled in the murky depths. Mouth opening, she choked on the muddy water, sinking farther away from the light above.

Just before she let go, accepting the finality of death, a hand caught her shirt sleeve, pulling her up.

Her mother's face was the first thing Billie saw as she broke the surface, bruised and oozing with fresh blood. Water gushed from her mouth in one long stream of muddy liquid. Her lungs rattled with every breath.

Uncle David reached out for Billie with his long, pointed nails, missing her face by inches. Candice grabbed his ratty hair, pulling him back as her hands enclosed around his throat. She fought with everything she had left.

They fell at the water's edge, her brother beating Candice down, fists pounding her body. He snatched up a rock in his fury, plunging it into her skin, the sound of flesh ripping with every blow.

Candice's screams pierced the night, as sharp as the rock he stabbed into her.

Billie's fingers trailed through the sand, searching for anything she could use. Leaves, sticks, the withered bone of an animal. Her fingers brushed against something sharp.

A long, jagged rock.

She threw it through the air faster than she could blink.

The rock hit him square in the face. The weapon dropped from his fingers. Blood poured from his crushed nose.

He licked his cracked lips, eyes gleaming like a madman, and lunged for Billie, hands tightening around her throat.

Billie sputtered for air. Her hands flailed through the air helplessly, feet kicking outward, twitching like a fish out of water. Her uncle's blood dripped into her eyes.

A deafening sound shattered the night. Uncle David's body fell away on the sand. Blood streamed from a hole in his head.

Billie backed away into the trees, ragged breaths whistling in her throat. Her right ear rang with a continuous, sharp pitch of sound.

Billie's eyes were locked on her uncle's lifeless form. She retched, the burning acid spewing onto a bush. It felt like tiny rocks were trapped in her esophagus, cutting her every time she breathed.

Candice stepped into view, the gun clasped in her bloody hands. She spotted Billie, taking a shaky step forward. Her body swayed. The gun dropped onto the ground as her mother toppled onto the sand.

Billie rushed to her, stumbling as her feet meshed into the soil, pushing through her pain with all the strength she had in her.

"Mama," she breathed, falling by her side. "Mama!"

The blood clung to her mother like a thick coat of paint. The ground was splattered with the liquid, like long, dirty strokes on white canvas. Her body sputtered with every breath. The life was seeping out of her, mixing with the water, lost with the tide.

"Look at me," her mother whispered.

Blood trickled down Candice's lip, blotting up on the sand.

"Look. At. Me."

"I don't know what to do," Billie cried, the tears obscuring her mother's image as they swelled in her eyes.

"You can't leave me. You can't."

Billie blinked back the tears, holding her mother's face in her scratched hands. "Please."

A word formed on her lips. She sputtered again, blood clogging her nose, gushing from her mouth.

"Mama."

She'd seen someone die before. Watched as Robert Smith took his last rattling breath. But she'd never seen anything like this.

Billie nestled into her mother's arms. It was just like the night Candice returned to her, drifting away into sleep as she fit like a puzzle piece in her mother's perfect hold.

"Goodnight, my dandelion," Candice whispered.

Then, her body shuddering for the final time, all was still.

. . . .

Billie's eyes opened. She'd heard her name. It almost sounded like it came from...

"Billie."

A woman stood over her. Blond hair spilled over her

shoulders and her piercing blue eyes were like a dream in themselves.

"Mama?"

She pulled herself up, but a gentle hand forced her back down. She could barely make out the stranger's words from the sharp ringing in her ear, like the high-pitch of a whistle. "Stay here. Help is on its way."

The dull throb of sirens droned on in the distance. Flashing lights pulsed through the trees.

"I thought you were…"

"It's me, Billie. It's Ginger."

"Mama…?"

"No. She's gone. I'm sorry."

Tears welled up in her eyes again. Her tongue was coated with a sour film. She swallowed, but it didn't get rid of the taste. Flies hovered over where she lay, as she gazed at the lifeless form in her arms. If she lay here long enough, maybe she wouldn't have to be saved.

"M-Mick…" she sputtered. "You have to find him… my uncle tried to—"

"They're okay, Billie," the woman whispered. "They

made it."

They made it.

Billie's eyes stung with salt. Tears poured from her face like blood from a wound.

Ginger picked Billie up in her arms, even though she'd told Billie to stay…not to get up…not to leave her mother…

"Let me go!" Billie cried. "I can't leave her! I can't…*I promised…*"

"She's gone, Billie," the cop said again, her words so soft she could barely hear them. "She's not here anymore."

Billie fell limp in Ginger's arms, staring up at her calming face, one just like her mother's. Sleep pressed on her eyes. She muttered one last word as she realized how perfectly she fit in Ginger's arms.

"Mama."

27
REALITY

BILLIE SLEPT AS the ambulance carried her away. If she would've opened her eyes, she might've seen the tears falling down Ginger's face; might have felt the cop's hand lying on top of her own.

"Stay with me," Ginger whispered, but her words were lost to the wail of the sirens.

Still, Billie slept. When she awoke, maybe she would be fortunate enough to forget.

. . . .

Billie stayed a night in the hospital. "Kept for observation," as she would later know. The nurses worried she might be in traumatic shock.

Besides, with the multiple wounds to her face, a broken nose, a mild concussion, and a sprained ankle, she wasn't in any condition to return home.

She slept mostly, drifting in and out of reality, blurred images lurking at the edge of her fuzzy vision. The whirring of the machines set her at ease.

She slept, unaware of the world. She didn't dream.

....

The light was a blinding brightness, stinging her eyes like a knife stabbed deep into her sockets.

"Where...where am I?"

Billie pushed a messy strand of hair off her face. The room spun.

"You're home now. You're okay."

Home?

A form sat in a chair by the doorway. The sun spilled into the room through the long veil of curtains.

"Can't you remember?" a soft, trembling voice asked.

She thought...her mind tugging...pulling at a distant memory.

She was in Ginger's house.

"You were discharged yesterday."

The bedsprings moaned beside her. A hand stroked her cheek.

"Are you feeling okay?"

Billie sucked in a long, quivering breath. She realized she could hear everything Ginger said, without having to strain to get a grasp on the words. The ringing in her ear was gone.

"Yeah…I'm…I'm fine," she said, drawing back at the cop's touch.

The recollection was there, the realization of it all making a tight knot form in her chest. It seemed to wrap around her organs, squeezing and constricting them, crushing her lungs every time she dared to breathe.

"How'd you find me?" Billie asked. "Make me remember."

Ginger sighed. "Your dad called. Alerted us that something was wrong. The medics rushed to meet him and I…I left to find you."

Billie nodded. "Okay," she whispered, the word itself hurting her where it shouldn't. Making it an effort to just *be*.

"She's dead, Ginger. She's gone. And I...I couldn't save her."

"It's not your fault. None of this will ever be your fault."

Billie squeezed her eyes shut. She turned away. "You look just like her."

Ginger didn't speak.

"Sometimes, I even think you *are* her."

"Billie—"

"And I don't want to think that. I can't help it. I just do."

"Billie."

She turned, staring deep into the cop's eyes. She didn't think she breathed at all.

"It's going to get better. Things will change, if you allow them to."

"I know, Ginger." She shuddered, a sob forcing its way out before she could stop it. "But what if they don't?"

. . . .

Billie opened the door to her dad's hospital room. Ginger waited outside in the hall.

"Dad?"

The room was dark. A monitor beeped in the corner.

Her dad's eyes flicked open. He sat up in the bed, cracking a smile. "What's up, squirt?"

Billie cut to the chase. "What did the doctor say?"

"Ahh, it was nothing. Said it was healing. Should be out in a week."

Billie returned the smile. "That's good."

"What about you?" His eyebrows raised. "Ginger treatin' you okay?"

Billie nodded. She guessed he already knew. "I'm staying with her at night. When she goes to work, I have to stay in the lobby. There's a woman—lady named Miss Nance—that watches me while Ginger works."

His eyes fell to the floor. "That Ginger—she's a nice woman. I'll have to let her know that, too."

"Dad?" Billie stood up. Her legs trembled. "I just

want you to come home."

"I know, baby. I will."

"And I don't know how we're going to do it, but we have to move on." She chewed her lip. "We have to start over."

"Why is that?"

She swallowed. "Because I won't be able to live if we don't."

His eyes flicked back to hers. "Okay."

"Mom would want that. Wouldn't she?"

Her dad closed his eyes. "Yeah, she would. She would."

"And I can't pretend either. Mom changed a long time ago. We should accept that."

A tear escaped down his cheek. "Okay," he mumbled.

Billie sat beside him on the bed. She rested a hand on his. "Can you do that for me, dad?"

He was shaking now. His head was turned away, so she couldn't see him. But she had never seen him more.

"I'll remember the way she used to smile," Billie

whispered. "I'll remember how she used to always call me her dandelion before she turned the light out. I'll remember our trips to the field behind the house. And her smile. God, that smile. I think I'll miss it more than anything."

Tears were pouring now, falling away onto the sheets. "I'll remember," she said, "because why would I forget?"

She shook her head. "I'm going to miss her, Dad."

"We all will," he said, his words trembling. "But I'm not going anywhere." He smiled, his eyes meeting her own. "Nowhere at all."

28

THE LOST AND THE FOUND

IT WAS THE middle of the day when the walls started to break in a house on Bentley Street. They caved in, withering away to dust and plaster. In its place, a new home was rebuilt and a different story began. This time, the memories wouldn't be locked away. They wouldn't be hidden, either.

This time, when the cars drove by and the people stopped to stare, the Johnsons would be there. This home would beat with a different heart, would hold proof of a different tale.

These Johnsons were here to stay. They weren't going

anywhere.

On the day the walls rose, new life began. On the day they rose, a house became a home.

Clara watched from the street. Her wounds no longer burned nor bled. She'd survived, and she would continue to, as long as the memories stayed within reach.

"We couldn't let them forget," she whispered. Beside her, her brother nodded.

"Y'all aren't ready for the tour of homes yet."

Clara laughed. The homeless man—or James, as he'd rather be called—stared at the place with a light burning behind his eyes.

"Thanks for the help."

"When ya gonna start my room out in the doghouse?"

"It's not a doghouse," Clara said, rolling her eyes. "It's a barn."

. . . .

They worked until sundown. Sweat dripped off of their backs and onto the parched dirt.

The barn was almost complete.

Clara was still getting over her fear of them. She could stand it as long as she could spot an open door.

James stayed behind to finish the roof. He nailed in the last of the wooden boards, leaning back to stare at the star-speckled sky through the cracks.

"Thanks for givin' me a home," he whispered.

"Anytime," Mick said. He followed after his sister, her pale, translucent skin burning through the dark.

Clara gained speed, laughter ringing throughout the night. It'd turned into a game.

"Come find me," she called, racing across the yard, a white blur against the towering pines.

Mick stopped to catch his breath. He plopped himself down on the grass, staring up at the shimmering lights in the night sky; at the billions of worlds flickering and fading like a flame.

He thought of Clara. A captive. Once bound, yet now free to see the light of day.

James. A prisoner by his past. Given a place to stay by a woman who reminded him of the daughter he'd lost.

And himself. A life built on a lie. A picture, shifting in and out of focus.

Staring up at the sky, his mind lost among it all, he thought of everything they'd become.

Free.

Safe.

Found.

....

James rung the bell at the front desk of the large police station. He'd changed into a suit. Washed away his dirt and grime and watched as it flooded down the drain.

Today was a special day.

"Ma'am, I need to talk with Ginger," James said, in his typical southern drawl.

The woman at the desk tilted her head. Her nametag read Miss Nance.

"I'm sorry, sir. She's quite busy. Have you made an appointment?"

Beside him, Clara stiffened.

"Naw, it'll be fine. I guess I can come back later."

Mick watched as Clara tugged on his arm, her eyes boring into Miss Nance's large, wrinkled face.

"This is very important. That's his *daughter* in there."

Miss Nance's eyebrows raised. "I'm sorry, but rules are rules. Either have an appointment or you don't."

"I don't have time for this," Clara muttered under her breath. She turned on her heel, tugging James along, as she hurried down the hallway where the officer's chambers were.

Mick smirked at Miss Nance. "I'm sorry. She doesn't take orders very well."

The woman's smile turned into a scowl. She scuttled away behind them. "I could have you arrested for this," she mumbled as Mick raced ahead to find his sister before Miss Nance did.

They were standing in the doorway to Ginger's office.

"Go," Mick heard Clara say.

He entered behind them, in the process of closing the door when Miss Nance's large, plump hand caught it from the other side.

"Stop right there," the large woman sputtered, clearly out of breath. "I'm calling security."

Ginger stood from her desk. Her mouth dropped. "Miss Nance, what's going on here?"

"I'm sorry, Miss Ginger, but they—"

"Leave it to me."

Miss Nance's face twisted. Her flabby chin shook as she talked. "What?"

"I'll take it from here."

The woman looked as though she'd just been fired. "Alright, then," she mumbled, skulking away back to her desk.

Mick grabbed Clara's arm. Maybe this wasn't such a good idea…

"Dad?" Ginger's eyes glistened in the pale, golden light.

"Hey, baby," he smiled. "I know. I'm hard to look at."

She didn't laugh. She didn't even say another word.

James wrapped her up in his arms, stroking her hair as the tears fell.

Mick took Clara's hand. He squeezed it in silent victory.

Some things went beyond words.

29
ONE LAST WISH

CANDICE HAGEN WAS gone, but that didn't mean she wasn't still here. Billie thought of her daily, when the sun rose on the field of dandelions, and when she lay in the darkness of her room at night, footsteps easing up the stairs like a whisper.

She thought of her when the rain thudded against the windows; when the lightning forked across the sky and set the world ablaze. She remembered the way Candice used to hold her during a storm. She'd never felt safer than when she was in her mother's arms.

And when she opened the door to her dad's room,

turning the key in the lock, her mother was everywhere all at once.

The boxes were no longer there. The key wasn't hidden away beneath the porch anymore.

There wasn't a need to store everything up like they used to. No, there wouldn't ever be a need for that again.

They were moving on, slowly but surely, even with the charges still filed against her dad.

John Hagen plead guilty to perjury in exchange for a plea deal a week after he was discharged from the hospital. He wouldn't get any jail time, but would have a short probation. This way, he could still be with Billie.

The news was expected; her dad would accept the crime. He would do what his wife didn't. This way, he could move on.

Now, pulling back the cover of her mother's journal, Billie read the last entry. It was written a day before she'd died.

My Dandelion,

Some see a weed, others see a wish.

To find peace, you have to accept life as it is—rather than as you would like it to be. I've had to learn this the hard way, making excuses and telling lies at the cost of losing it all. I couldn't accept life. Instead, I tried to run away from it.

Patience is the key to it all, Billie. Take time to catch the beautiful glimpses God gives us of our world. On days like this, times like this, it's easy to succumb to hatred, even when there's so much hope blooming just outside your window. Even though I may not always be around to tell you so, don't let this stop you from living your dream and focusing on the simple moments life has to offer. Blink, and you'll miss it. Turn away, and you'll never even know it's there.

Until next time,

Candice

Billie stared down at the words, trying to understand it all, trying to breathe it in and *taste* it.

It was only in doing so that she could finally let her go.

. . . .

285

Billie stood in the field behind her house. The sun spilled through the clouds, leaking its warmth on the clearing. The air seemed to glimmer with hope.

If pushed to the limit, she was capable of anything. Her mother had harbored guilt, shame, even contemplated murder. That hadn't made her any less of a human than anyone else.

Even though such actions had led to her end, Billie would have to look past that. Her mother was right—there was beauty in everything, even within herself.

She lifted a dandelion to her lips, making one final wish.

She watched it drift away, lost on the wind.

Fading. Fading.

Gone.

30

DON'T LOOK BACK

CHAPEL HILL CEMETERY swarmed with visitors. The rain was a downpour, running off of the canvas tent where the Hagen family gathered. If someone was looking for a sign, God provided one.

Through Mr. Abram's never-ending prayer, Mick watched a girl slide out from underneath the tent and step into the rain.

Billie.

The water drenched the soles of Mick's dress shoes as he slipped away from the crowd, following after her. He thought, through the haze, he could make out her figure walking through the tombstones. Her back was turned to him, arms crossed over her chest. Her wet hair clung to her skin, spread down the folds of her back.

Mick stopped close enough to touch her. Standing there, she looked oddly peaceful, like something out of place against the backdrop of a thousand graves.

When Billie turned, she seemed to look right through him, like he wasn't there.

"You know, I couldn't have ever done any of this without you."

The rain subsided, the final drops sliding away down the marble and dripping on the colored stone.

Mick started to speak, but something in her tone made him stop.

Her eyes met his. She wasn't smiling.

"But it doesn't matter anymore. My mother is dead."

A knot formed in Mick's chest. His voice came out flat. "I can't even imagine…"

"Your mother is dead, too, if you've forgotten."

Mick's teeth bit down hard on his bottom lip. "Billie."

"But you won't ever know how that feels. Your mother didn't even know you. And you never knew her."

"Why are you doing this?" Mick choked. "Why are you *like* this?"

"And now your sister lives, while my mother…" She clenched her jaw. Tears brimmed in her blue eyes. "It isn't fair. None of it is fair."

"Do you think I wanted this? That I wanted my family to die?" Mick was almost screaming. "And if you can remember, I had a woman who loved me. Who died when I was six. All out of hate. All because of a man who let greed overpower love. That's what you're doing now, Billie. Hate has blinded you to where you can't even recognize a friend. Don't give in to it. I can't lose someone else because of it."

"Hate?" Billie snorted. "This isn't hate. It's *life*. Things change. We move on. We cut out everyone who thinks different."

"So it's me? I'm the one who reminds you of your mother. I'm the one who makes you remember." He stepped closer, grabbing her arm before she could turn away. "But you remind me of a lot of things. Things I wished would stay buried. But it doesn't matter...don't you realize that? You're all I have left."

Billie closed her eyes. Her words were strained. "Death follows you, Mick. No else needs to die. Not for me."

"That's it then? This is goodbye?"

Billie snatched her arm out of his grip, backing away. She stared at him as if she'd never seen him before; like he'd never been her friend, but only something to use. Mick hated the way it made him feel.

"Yes."

She sighed. For a moment, he thought she would change her mind...that she wouldn't leave...not *him*. But when she spoke, all his hopes slipped away.

"My mother made me realize that, sometimes, we have to escape the things that threaten to sink us. And that's what I need. Some time away from it all. From you.

"Can't you see?" she said, like it was the simplest thing in the world. "Together, we're dangerous. Apart, we're safe."

"What about our promise?"

She shook her head. "It never meant anything." Her eyes fell from his. "It was never real."

"Go," Mick gritted. "Leave. Act like I care. Because I don't."

She nodded. "Bye, Mick."

He watched her go, his heart shattering a little more with every step she took. He wanted to stop her—tell her she was the only thing that had kept him going, the only thing that gave him a reason to live.

But how could he explain that when everyone in his life decided to leave?

"Never say goodbye," he whispered. If she heard him, she didn't show it. She never looked back.

EPILOGUE

A LIGHT FLICKERED on in the kitchen window, the last house along the end of the street.

David Evans twisted the faucet in the sink, splashing a cool stream of water on his face. His sandy blond hair was tousled to the side, ruffled in a wad on his head. Dark patches beneath his eyes held proof of a restless night.

The gentle snores of his family drifted down the stairs. Jessica and Olivia were asleep in their beds.

A drop of rain hit the window glass. Lightning flashed outside, illuminating the trees bordering the lawn. Claps of thunder resonated through the night air.

Storm clouds were rolling in, swallowing the stars.

Rain fell in torrents from the sky, a steady rhythm pelting the glass.

David's hand hovered over the light switch as his eyes detected movement from the trees.

Against the drenched, night sky, he thought he saw a figure watching from the woods.

But when he blinked, it was gone.

To see how it ends
Read Book 4 of the Summersville series
Hidden Places
Arriving 2020

ACKNOWLEDGEMENTS

As always, there are so many people to thank.

First and foremost, I could never write a book worthy enough to publish if it weren't for each and every one of my beta readers: Tara Manson, Hope Allen, Olivia Garrett, Jessica Rockett, Jill Stevenson, Tammy Cosson, Emily Casey, and Olivia J. Bennett. Thank you all for your time and effort on every single draft I throw your way!

To my parents, for hauling me around to all the different events, festivals, and signings when you could be doing anything else. Mom, thank you for always being an unwavering source of guidance and inspiration, and for always being so honest and committed when it comes to publishing a new book. No one truly understands the amount of hard work and dedication it takes to getting one of my novels from idea to print, but you. I love you. Dad, thank you for always listening to my crazy ideas, pitches, and understanding better than anyone when I need to kill off a character (which, is quite often). I love you.

Continuous thanks to Chipola College for reaching out and inviting me on campus to speak to prospective teachers about my books and the impact they have on their students, as well as the many other schools, libraries, and clubs that have welcomed me to speak.

To my street team, for spreading the word about *Buried Truths* and helping get this installment into the hands of readers. Whenever a new cover, announcement, or release date is in the works, I can always count on you!

Kelly Harrington, you have been so helpful in getting my books in stores and on the shelves. Thank you for always recommending me to any B&N customer in need of a thriller and helping get my name out there.

To all the fellow teen authors and writers I've had the pleasure of connecting with on Instagram and Twitter: Olivia J. Bennett, Blaise Ramsay, Hannah Kay, Brian McBride, Brittney Kristina, Erin Forbes, Nina Martineck (The Knowers), Olivia Scott, and Mckenzie Wagner to name a few. You'll never begin to understand how much you've impacted my dreams, but also me as a person.

To Olivia J. Bennet and Janelle Mainero, for providing blurbs for this book.

Fisher's Pharmacy and McLean's Florist—thank you for always keeping a number of my works in stock at your stores.

As always, many thanks to my editor, Josh Vogt, and my formatter, Whitney Evans.

To God, for all the blessings I've received.

Finally, to all the young, aspiring writers—don't let anyone tell you that your age defines you. Dreams never come with an age limit, nor do they expire. Make a name for yourself. Continue honing your skills. The rest will be history.

ABOUT THE AUTHOR

McCaid Paul is 16 years old and lives on a farm in a rural community in Northwest Florida. He enjoys hiking, traveling, and spending time with family. In first grade, he learned to journal, which developed into a love of writing. McCaid is an avid fan of anything crime or mystery. *Buried Truths* is his third novel.

Check him out on his website

www.mccaidpaulbooks.com

Instagram @mccaidpaul

Facebook @MccaidP

Twitter @MccaidP

Twitter @summersville1 for book updates